MW01342625

Puzzled

Keith Cole

AuthorHouse™
1663 Liberty Drive, Suite 200
Bloomington, IN 47403
www.authorhouse.com
Phone: 1-800-839-8640

First published by AuthorHouse 10/18/2007

ISBN: 978-1-4343-2709-3 (sc)

Library of Congress Control Number: 2007906665

Printed in the United States of America
Bloomington, Indiana

This book is printed on acid-free paper.

To the girls in my life – Debbie, Jessie, and Sophie.
Dream big and hold on tight.

Contents

The Family Secret

The Exeter Boarding School campus sits on a rise of low, rolling hills beside the Thomas River. The river is broad and quiet as it calmly slides past the school in a series of wide, looping turns on its way through the valley. The water is cold and clean though it is stained brown by the tannins that wash into the river from the surrounding forests. But it is a copper-colored brown rather than a muddy brown and the river creates a pleasant contrast to the deep-green canopy of the trees that covers the hills.

The Exeter campus has been around for so long that it is now part of the forest. The grayish-white limestone of the buildings has darkened over the years and the buildings look like large piles of rocks, their rectangular shapes hidden by trees and by the ivy clinging to the walls. The trees are thick and old and most, especially the oaks, are taller than the buildings and give the school a look of quiet permanence and old age. And in fact the campus is old, built in the 1790's by an Englishman named Oliver Easton who had come to the American Colonies before the Revolutionary War. Easton was a well-educated, hard-working man and started a tea company and a lumber business which quickly grew and made him quite wealthy. He was also an amateur naturalist and his vast wealth allowed him ample free time to spend along the Thomas River in pursuit of new specimens of plants and birds. He ultimately decided to leave his business affairs to others and left Boston to build a large mansion on the hills overlooking the river so that he could spend more time on his biology studies. When the Revolutionary War came Easton remained loyal to the King of England and his mansion was destroyed in a mysterious fire, most likely set by American colonists fighting the English but possibly accidental. With his mansion gone and his businesses ruined by the war Easton decided to leave New England and moved to South Carolina where he subsequently made another fortune selling cotton.

By the end of the war Easton was in his late forties, very wealthy, and still unmarried. This changed one evening when, at a lavish dinner banquet, he was introduced to Rebecca Stanton, the daughter of an old friend from New England. She was beautiful, quiet, and intelligent and six months later they were married. Their marriage was long and happy, the happiness broken only by an inability to have children. Frustrated by their childlessness, they slowly managed to overcome their emptiness through a shared love of books and learning and over the years a plan slowly took shape, a plan that would put their love of books and learning and children together in one place. In 1794 Oliver Easton and his wife Rebecca sold their cotton business and took their fortune back to the banks of the Thomas River in New England. High on the banks above the river they built a school, a school as good as any of the great boarding schools of England.

Izzy Watson knew the whole story. By now she knew it by heart, knew more about Exeter Boarding School than any of the eighty-one new freshman due to arrive tomorrow for the start of school. After all, Izzy was the fifth, and last, person in her family to attend Exeter. Her mother, Anne Elise Montrose Watson, had been the first, a graduate of the Class of 1977 and also the class president and class valedictorian of the Class of '77. Izzy's older sister Elizabeth was valedictorian of the Class of 2001 and her brother Robert was Homecoming King and class vice-president of the Class of 2003. Her other brother Charles was starting his senior year, presently third in his class but determined to be the next, and most likely last, member of the Watson family to be the valedictorian at Exeter Boarding School.

Isabella Marie Watson was a Watson through- and – through. Like the rest of the family she was intelligent, polite, well-spoken, well-traveled, and sophisticated. She knew a salad fork from a dinner fork, knew that nice young ladies didn't cross their legs, could fold a napkin correctly, and knew not to wear white after Labor Day. She could speak French, recite poems by Robert Frost, play the violin and piano, and separate the works of Mozart or Beethoven or Strauss after hearing only eight or ten notes. She had traveled to New York and Boston, as well as to Paris, London, Madrid, and Stockholm. There was certainly little doubt among anyone at Exeter Boarding School that another of the famous Watson's was coming.

But Izzy had some doubts. In fact, she had quite a few. But then again, didn't she always? Isabella Watson may have been what she was but it certainly wasn't who she was. A Watson yes, but Izzy Watson, and to be Izzy was something quite different than being Isabella. Not better or worse but most assuredly and uniquely different. It had always been that way. At first her mother had tried to fight it, had tried to make an Isabella out of her Izzy. But it was a struggle. Even as a toddler Izzy wouldn't answer to the name "Isabella" and her mother had to finally give up in frustration and call her "Izzy," at least when other people weren't around. Worse even than the battles over her name were the battles over her clothes. No one ever managed to invent a fastening device from which the young Izzy could not escape. Buckles, zippers, belts, laces, velcro, snaps, tape, glue. Nothing could keep unwanted shoes or clothes on the child. She was the first Watson in three generations to play outside barefooted, indeed was one of only a few Watson's who had ever wanted to play outside at all, shoed or unshoed.

But her mother kept at it. She learned through trial and error that if she wrote "Izzy" on the tags of the child's clothes that she could usually get her to wear "nice" clothes, even on rare occasions to wear a dress.

Unfortunately for Anne Elise Montrose Watson her youngest daughter was quite intelligent and adaptable in addition to being a bit head-strong and stubborn. So by the time Izzy was ten she and Anne had learned the art of compromise. Izzy would wear the lace-trimmed floral dress and the bow in her hair if, and only if, on Saturday she could wear whatever she wanted. This bargaining arrangement worked out well for both Izzy and her mother. During the week her mother got her sweet, pretty, well-mannered Isabella and on weekends Izzy got to be Izzy.

It was a good system and became the perfect system once Anne Elise learned to close her eyes when Izzy came down the stairs on Saturday morning on her way out the door. Saturday was a chance for Izzy to make a fashion statement, a statement that very clearly said "I'm Izzy." All week long she wore matching outfits- A red skirt with matching red shoes and a pink bow; a black skirt with black shoes and a starched white blouse. But on Saturdays nothing Izzy wore matched, except occasionally her shoes. She wore whatever she felt like wearing and had no problem pairing striped pants with a polka-dot shirt or brown boots with shorts. A typical outfit might consist of a red baseball cap with a yellow shirt, blue pants, and black and white high-top sneakers. Izzy didn't have many clothes of her own besides a collection of dresses, skirts, and blouses so she was forced to borrow clothes from her older siblings. Most of what she wore was several sizes too big for her but this posed no problem for Izzy. She simply rolled-up the pant legs and pinned them or tucked them into her boot tops. Shirt tails were tied in a knot at her waist or left to dangle around her knees. She stuffed socks into the toes of her brothers' shoes so they would fit, put rubber bands around her shirt sleeves, and made her own set of suspenders out of a pair of red shoe laces.

Izzy marched around the neighborhood every Saturday looking like she had been blindfolded and forced to pick her clothes off the rack at a second-hand store. Her appearance was a neighborhood scandal and was truly shocking for a member of the sophisticated and straight-laced Watson family. But her friends understood it even if their parents didn't. The parents usually stood by looking bewildered and uncomfortable each time the multi-colored and untidy young Watson girl appeared. Izzy's friends would simply look up at their parents, shrug their shoulders, and say "T J I S D," a signal of understanding and acceptance- "That's just Izzy. She's different."

The abbreviated phrase "TJISD" was certainly an accurate description of Izzy's Saturday morning wardrobe but it went far deeper. For TJISD described most everything about Izzy Watson, especially when it came to being a member of the Watson family. She took voice lessons like all Watsons did but sang swinging little jazz songs that she made up herself. She played the violin but jammed on it like a fiddle and slapped the piano keys like she was putting out a fire. And Izzy was an out-and –out tomboy, an unheard of and most un- Watson-like behavior. She could easily outrun her older brothers and could hit harder, throw farther, jump higher, and swim further than all but two of the boys in her neighborhood. Izzy was the best kickball player at school and was great at soccer, hockey, volleyball, basketball, and even football. Despite the protests of her distraught and worried mother she liked dirt, bugs, dogs, cats, hamsters and almost every other animal and could do five different bird calls. TJISD.

Izzy acted and dressed differently than other girls her age and certainly unlike any member of the Watson family ever had. But there was something else about Izzy that was different. It was something that made her friends wonder and their parents shake their heads, something that made her mother worry and her teachers confused, but it wasn't something anyone could see. Izzy's most peculiar trait was not an external one but rather an internal one, a certain something on the inside that when it came to the outside struck others as unusual and quirky. It was her personality, her individuality, and her independence that really set Izzy apart from everyone else. It came out in how she dressed and in how she acted but it was Izzy's inner spirit that made her unique.

It took a while even for her mother to figure out that there was an Izzy inside the beautiful, wide-eyed little girl she had named Isabella. The battle over clothes wasn't that unusual she thought; lots of parents had trouble getting toddlers to wear clothes, though it had never happened in the Watson family before.

Mrs. Watson only truly began to understand the day she came home to find eight-year-old Isabella with a bright white stripe of paint down the middle of her long black hair. The sight of it was shock enough but her young daughter's explanation was what really got her attention. Isabella calmly explained that she was tired of her brothers and kids at school bothering her all the time. She thought about trying to beat them up but she knew that wouldn't work. So she sat outside at recess and thought about how she could get people to leave her alone and the perfect idea came to her. A skunk! Nobody ever bothers a skunk. It was the perfect solution. So she came right home after school and painted a long white skunk-stripe in her hair.

Over time Mrs. Watson got over the skunk incident but Link was another matter altogether. She first met Link when Isabella was ten but Izzy had known him for years. It happened when Mrs. Watson went upstairs to put some laundry away in the boys' room. As she walked down the hallway she overheard Isabella in her bedroom talking to someone. A bit confused, since no one else was home, she opened the door to the bedroom and found Isabella sitting cross-legged on the floor, alone.

"Who are you talking to?," Mrs. Watson asked.

"What?" Izzy replied, surprised by her mother's sudden entrance.

"I heard you talking to someone," she said. "Who was it?"

Izzy thought for a moment. Should she tell her or not? Izzy didn't want her mom to freak out but on the other hand she didn't want to lie either, so she decided now was as good a time as any to tell her about Link. "I was talking to Link," she answered.

"Link?," Mrs. Watson said. "I don't see anyone in here. Do you have another one of your creatures with you? What is it? A hamster? A mouse?"

Izzy chuckled as her mother stepped backward, her eyes wide as she held the laundry basket out in front of her for protection. "Relax mom," Izzy said, "I don't have any animals up here. Link is my friend."

Mrs. Watson stood still for a moment. Her ten-year old daughter had an imaginary friend? That was fine for a four-year-old but not for a ten-year-old. "Is Link your imaginary friend?" she asked calmly.

"If by "imaginary" you mean "made-up and not real" than no, Link is not my imaginary friend," Izzy replied. "If you mean "invisible," than yes."

Mrs. Watson fought to remain calm. "Why do you call him Link?" she asked.

"Because he is my link to the other side," Izzy said.

"What other side, Isabella?" her mother asked softly.

"You know mom," Izzy said, "the other side, that place we can all go when we need to figure things out or get some advice or just relax. Kind of a place to take your mind for a walk."

Confused, and more than a little worried, Mrs. Watson flashed a nervous smile. "Okay honey, I understand," she said and slowly backed out of the room.

Mrs. Watson spent the next few days searching the internet in a near-desperate attempt to find out what was wrong with Isabella. Unable to find an answer she sought advice from her husband, her family, and her friends. Unsatisfied with their answers she took Isabella to the doctor to make sure that she didn't have some awful disease. Next she tried the minister and followed that with a visit to the school psychologist for a thorough examination.

It was unanimous. Everyone agreed that Isabella wasn't odd or weird or goofy. She didn't have a brain tumor, wasn't infected, and showed no signs of toxic exposure to lead or mercury. She wasn't crazy, possessed by demons, addicted to drugs, or in any way mentally ill. Her parents, their friends, their family, the doctor, the minister, and the school psychologist all agreed. There was nothing wrong with Isabella Marie Watson. She was just Izzy. TJISD.

But all of that was in the past and now even Izzy knew things were about to change. She was almost fourteen-years-old and tomorrow she would be leaving for boarding school. She wasn't particularly scared to go to Exeter. Her brothers and her sister had told her all about it so she knew what to expect. But knowing what to expect and being prepared for it didn't stop Izzy from worrying. Could she make new friends? Would the other students accept her? She knew the type of kids that went to Exeter Boarding School- prissy, a bit stuck-up, hyper-competitive. And then there was the school itself. Uniforms all week, a list of rules a mile long, and no dogs or dirt or bugs or music. There was nothing about Exeter Boarding School or the students who went there that fit Izzy's style. Nothing!

"Izzy! Izzy!" The sound of her mother's voice jolted Izzy out of her thoughts.

"Yea mom," she yelled, "I'm out here on the porch."

"Could you please come in the kitchen," her mother called. "Your father and I would like to talk to you."

Izzy got up off the porch swing and walked into the house. Her mom and dad were sitting at the kitchen table, each holding a cup of coffee, and they looked uncomfortable. Izzy knew this look and this setting very well. Her parents usually did this when she was in trouble or was about to get a lecture.

"Sit down honey," her dad said calmly. "We need to talk to you about something."

Izzy slipped into a chair and waited for one of them to speak, unsure of what she might have done wrong.

"Isabella," her mother began, "we need to tell you something. Perhaps we should have told you earlier or maybe we shouldn't even tell you now. We aren't really sure what's right. But this does seem like the right time with your going away to Exeter. You know how kids can be in high school."

"Mom," Izzy groaned, "this isn't another lecture about sex is it?"

"Isabella!" her mother exclaimed, "it is about no such thing, though perhaps we do need to talk about that again."

Izzy's father softly patted his wife's arm. "Anne, let me have a try at it," he said. He shifted his chair and looked at Izzy. "Honey, this is difficult for your mother and I. We love you very much and we don't want to upset you. But time is forcing our hand. You're going away tomorrow and starting a new phase of your life. People at Exeter know our family and have for years and a lot of people there know about it. We thought we should tell you before someone accidentally says something."

"Says something about what?," Izzy said. "What do they know?"

Her father looked straight at Izzy. "That you're adopted Isabella."

"I'm what?," Izzy cried. "Adopted?"

"We adopted you when you were just a little baby," her mother said softly.

Izzy stared at them. She didn't know what to say, didn't know what to think.

"I know this must be a terrible shock to you," her mother continued. "But please don't be upset. We love you dearly

Isabella. We always have and we always will. And please don't think that we love you in a different way or any less than Robert or Elizabeth or Charles. We love all of our children. We felt like we had to tell you before you went to Exeter. We were afraid someone might say something and you'd be terribly hurt and upset."

Izzy sat quietly as the reality of her parents words slowly sunk in. She was shocked, and a bit confused, but she wasn't particularly angry or upset. She knew her parents loved her and she loved them. But the bomb they had just dropped had exploded her world and left her mind a jumbled mess of questions and doubts. Izzy finally looked up at her parents and saw the worry and concern on their faces.

"It's okay you guys," she said. "I'm not gonna freak-out over this or anything. I know this was really hard for you but you don't need to worry about it. I know you love me and you know I love you. This doesn't change any of that. It's just, well, it's just kind of a shock and it brings up a lot of questions. Like, for example, "Who am I?"

"You're Isabella Marie Watson," her father answered proudly. "And we love you."

Izzy smiled at him. "Thanks Dad," she answered. "But I'm not Isabella. I'm Izzy and now I think I know why."

The three of them sat around the table for almost two hours as Izzy's parents answered what questions they could. They talked about when she was little and how she had tested them and about all of the wonderful times they had had and about the future. Her parents laughed and smiled, relieved that at last their secret was out and the weight of the world was off their shoulders. But some of that weight had fallen on Izzy. She was now the one with a secret and with questions about what to do with it.

Izzy was exhausted and they had to leave for school early in the morning. She got up from the table, kissed her parents good night, and went up to her room. As she layed in bed the questions and the doubts continued to swirl in her head. So it's true then she thought to herself. TJISD. I am different. But who am I ? She fell asleep long before the answers came.

A Rough Start

Izzy was tired. Her eyes would only open half-way and stung like they do after a day at the pool. She washed her face and squeezed in a few eye-drops but her eyes still looked swollen and red. She looked like she had been crying all night but she hadn't been, not even after what her parents had told her last night. But she'd had a long, restless night of sleep, tossing and turning most of the evening until her alarm finally went off at six o'clock. Tired or not she needed to get ready to leave for boarding school and her dad wanted to be on the road by seven-thirty.

Izzy brushed her long black hair and pulled it back in a ponytail with a red leather hair band with small white feathers that she had made herself. Exeter Boarding School wouldn't let her wear her favorite hair band during school but school didn't officially start until tomorrow so she figured she could wear what she wanted.

But Izzy also knew that her mother would freak if she wore anything too outrageous so she toned down the rest of her outfit. She pulled on a pair of white pants, one leg of which she had split to the knee and patched with a triangular piece of denim covered with yellow stars. She slipped on a tight yellow collar-less shirt and finally settled on wearing leather clogs with plain white socks.

Izzy walked across the room and looked at herself in the mirror. Her hair and her clothes looked fine even if her eyes didn't. She stood for a moment and studied her reflection. Her mother had just recently told her how she was beginning to look like a young woman but Izzy hadn't paid much attention to her. She had never thought much about things like that, had never worried about body image or her figure. Izzy didn't wear make-up and never wasted her time reading teen magazines with their obsessive focus on looks, fashion, boys, and beauty products. But as she stood in front of the mirror she felt a little different. She could see that her body had changed over the summer. She had grown almost three inches and was no longer skinny and clumsy-looking. Now she was tall, thin, and muscular and had a chest that wasn't easily hidden even by the baggy shirts she usually wore. She was, as her mother had said, more "shapely."

Izzy turned away from the mirror. She had enough to worry about today without bringing a bunch of "body-image" issues into it. That stuff didn't matter anyway. What mattered now was Exeter Boarding School and all the real worries that came along with it.

"Izzy?"

"Yea Dad!," Izzy answered.

"We've got to get going," he called from downstairs. "Hurry up and finish packing and then come on down."

"Okay," she answered.

Finish packing? She hadn't even started packing though that was not at all unusual. Izzy usually waited until the last minute to do most things, not because she was lazy or absent-minded but because she usually had other things on her mind. She always managed to get things done in time but her laid-back style drove her mother crazy. Her mother was, in Izzy's opinion, way too hung-up on schedules and planning and all it ever did was make her anxious and flustered. Izzy didn't get anxious and flustered, ever. She could plan and schedule when she wanted to but Izzy had her own concept of time and it wasn't easily measured with clocks or calendars.

Besides, there was no rush. Izzy could pack quickly since there wasn't much to pack. Exeter Boarding School required students to wear uniforms during the week so she only needed clothes for the weekends. She went over to her closet, pulled out a few pairs of her favorite pants and a few tops, and stuffed them in the suitcase. She filled the rest of the suitcase with socks, underwear, shoes, and toiletries and zipped it shut. Izzy was more careful about what she put in the leather shoulder bag. She packed several of her hand made necklaces and belts, a couple of hats, a family picture, and a few other things she didn't want to be without. Satisfied that she hadn't forgotten anything she closed the leather bag and flopped down on the bed beside it.

"Link," Izzy sighed, "good morning."

"Good morning Izzy," he replied.

"How am I going to get through this?," Izzy asked. "A new school. New people. And now this whole adoption thing!"

"Give it time," Link replied.

"Time?," Izzy exclaimed. "I don't have any time. I don't need any time. I need answers!"

"Good answers take time Izzy," Link said calmly.

"Fine," Izzy replied with an irritated tone. "Time. But what can I do now so I can get through today?"

"Fast," Link answered.

"Yes, fast," Izzy said. "My dad's waiting for me. I gotta go."

Link laughed. "No, Izzy," he said. "I mean FAST. Focus on what you have to do, have a good Attitude, Smile, and Try. FAST."

Izzy thought for a moment and then smiled, "FAST," she said. "Thanks Link."

"You're welcome, Izzy," he replied.

Izzy grabbed her bags, carried them downstairs and dropped them on the floor near the door. "I'm ready to go you guys!," she said loudly.

Her mother came out from the kitchen and gave Izzy a hug. "We can't go yet," she said. "You haven't even eaten. Come in the kitchen and sit down for a minute."

Izzy followed her into the kitchen and slid into a chair. She wasn't hungry but she loaded some pancakes onto her plate so she wouldn't hurt her mother's feelings. Pancakes were Izzy's favorite and she knew her mother had made them especially for her.

Her mother brought over a glass of milk and set it on the table next to Izzy. "How are you dear?," she asked softly.

Izzy looked up from her plate and noticed that her mother's eyes looked worse than her's had this morning, only for a different reason. She knew her mother had been crying.

Izzy smiled. "I'm fine mom," she said. "Don't worry about me. I'm not mad at you or anything. I'm just a little confused, that's all."

"I know you are Isabella," she replied. "I'm so sorry we had to tell you about the adoption right before you leave for Exeter. The timing is terrible but…."

"Mom," Izzy said, cutting her off, "it's okay. Really. We talked about it last night and I'm cool with it. I understand, I really do. Don't worry about it. Worrying doesn't do any good."

Her mother managed a weak smile. "Thanks Izzy," she said. "You're a special kid."

"I'm not a kid anymore Mom," Izzy replied. "I'm almost fourteen and I'm heading off to boarding school. It's time I grow up."

Izzy and her mother talked a while longer as her dad loaded the bags in the car. When he was done he joined them at the table and the three of them laughed and joked for almost an hour as they tried to hold onto what they all knew was Izzy's last morning of childhood. Reluctantly, they finally went out to the car and left for Exeter.

The trip to Exeter Boarding School usually took about three hours on the Maxwell Freeway but the three Watsons decided to take the back roads so they could spend a little more time together. The road was narrow and curvy, especially as it crossed up into the low-slung hills to the west. The trees were still thick and green except for a few sugar maples that were just beginning to show some color. Fall was coming early this year as it had been an abnormally cool summer and even in early September one could feel a change in the air. By late-morning the car topped Fitzpatrick's Hill and Izzy could see the buildings of Exeter Boarding School down below. The car slowly moved down the hill towards the campus and was soon parked under a large tree near a gate.

The campus was crawling with people. A large white tent stood in the courtyard next to a black and yellow sign that said "Welcome Freshman Class. Please Register Here." At least a hundred people were at the tent, standing in lines or talking in groups or shaking hands with the well-dressed teachers. Izzy's hands felt sweaty and her heart pounded as she stepped from the car. She quickly and silently spoke to Link as she followed her parents toward the tent.

"Anne Elise Watson!," an older woman cried as they walked into the tent. "Don't you just look fabulous!"

A large, well-dressed, important-looking woman embraced Mrs. Watson and kissed her cheek. "You don't look like you've aged a single day since you graduated."

Mrs. Watson straightened herself. "Thank you, Mrs. Thompkins," she said politely. "You look wonderful yourself. You remember my husband Ronald."

"I do. I do indeed," she answered as she shook his hand. "I remember him well." She turned and looked at Izzy. "And you are obviously Isabella. I am so glad to finally have you here at Exeter."

Izzy politely shook hands with Mrs. Thompkins who she knew was the principal of Exeter Boarding School.

Her mother had often talked about her as Mrs. Thompkins had been the principal when she was a student. Her sister and brothers had also told Izzy about Mrs. Thompkins, mainly to warn her that she was a stern and strict woman and to avoid her at all cost.

"Hello Principal Thompkins," Izzy answered politely.

"Welcome Isabella," she replied. "Welcome to Exeter. We are most pleased to have another member of the Watson family here at our school. I have little doubt that you will be as good a student and citizen as your older brothers and sister have been."

"I'll try Ma'am," Izzy responded.

Principal Thompkins squeezed Izzy's hand tightly between her own two large hands and looked at her.

"Indeed, I believe you will," she said. "Yes indeed."

Mrs. Thompkins called over a young, dark-haired teacher and instructed him to help Izzy with the registration process. Her parents stayed with the Principal while Izzy and the teacher slowly made their way through the maze of tables scattered around the tent. They filled out dozens of forms and Izzy had her picture taken for her school I.D. card. She read a four-page "Exeter Code of Conduct" booklet and signed a card saying that she had read it completely and would follow all the rules and regulations. She received her room key, library card, lunch ticket, and class schedule and then went to the school store where she bought three school uniforms. An hour later she returned to the tent where she quietly and reluctantly said goodbye to her parents.

Izzy stood on the sidewalk and watched as the car slowly moved off down the road until finally it disappeared around the corner. She gathered her suitcase and the plastic bag with her new uniforms and headed up the side-walk toward her dormitory house on the far east side of the campus. It was cool out, almost cold, as she made her way along the walk under the shade of the large oak trees. She saw a wooden park bench in a sunny spot near a statue and sat down, hoping to warm herself on the outside as well as on the inside.

"Link? Are you there?," Izzy asked softly.

"Of course I'm here Izzy," Link replied. "Good afternoon."

"Good afternoon," she replied. "So, what do you think?"

"About what?," Link asked.

"Come on Link!," Izzy protested. "You know what I mean. What do you think about Exeter, about this place?"

"It seems okay to me," he answered. "Beautiful trees. A lovely campus. A lot of nice people. It's wonderful."

Izzy sighed. "Then why does it feel like a jail to me? Pages of rules and regulations. Uniforms. A mean old principal. It's even got walls around it!"

"How do you know she's mean?," Link asked.

"Who?," Izzy replied.

"The principal," he answered.

"My brothers and my sister told me," Izzy said. "Everyone says she is really tough and mean."

"Well," Link said slowly "she seems quite pleasant to me. Don't be so quick to judge other people. And don't believe everything you hear."

"Okay, okay," Izzy said hurriedly, cutting him off. "No lectures today Link. Please. It's just weird, you know, being here all by myself."

"You're not by yourself, Izzy," Link replied.

"I know," Izzy said, "but you know what I mean. I've been here a hundred times and I know all about it. But it still feels kinda weird. Not creepy weird, just weird."

"New things are like that at first," Link said. "Just give it a little time."

Izzy was quiet for a moment, hoping that Link's words could push the doubts out of ther head. "Alright,"

she finally said. "I'll give it a try. But it still feels like a jail, like a weird jail."

"Maybe you should try to think positive instead of negative," Link said. "How about "It's a beautiful school with nice people" rather than "it's a weird jail?"

Izzy stood up and grabbed her bags. "Very well," she said, "you win again Link. Just give me a second to change my attitude and put a smile on my face."

"Atta girl Izzy!," Link said enthusiastically. "Have a great day!".

"Goodbye Link," she replied.

Izzy turned and headed towards her room in Franklin Hall, a large fieldstone building on the edge of campus and the second oldest building at Exeter Boarding School. The Easton Mansion was the oldest building and now served as housing for the principal and most of the teachers. Franklin Hall had been the original school building but as Exeter grew through the years new classrooms had been built and Franklin was made into a girls dormitory. Izzy had been there several times with her mother and her sister and to her it looked and felt like an old castle. The doors were thick and heavy, arched at the top, and nearly ten feet high. The floors in the hallway were made of limestone and were noisy and cold and the wooden floors in the rooms creaked with every step. Each room had only one small window which made the rooms seem darker and even smaller than they actually were.

Izzy stopped at the bottom of the large stone steps leading up to the front door of Franklin Hall. She had been dreading this moment for weeks. A cold, dark, noisy little room was not her style. In fact, it was the exact opposite of the warm, bright, colorful, and cozy room she had at home. But she didn't have a choice. She thought of Link and a weak little smile appeared on her lips. Izzy straightened herself, shifted the bag on her shoulder, and started up the steps. As she walked up the steps Izzy heard a noise off to the right. She turned her head to look and spotted a fat gray squirrel sitting upright on a branch as he clicked out an alarm call. Izzy watched as he continued to chatter loudly but unfortunately she forgot to watch the steps. Her left foot came up short and struck the front of the step. She tried to catch herself but it was too late. She dropped her suitcase as her arms instinctively stretched out to break her fall and it skidded noisily down the steps. Her shoulder bag twisted as she fell and wrapped itself around her neck as she landed face-first on the steps, her left hand squarely in the middle of a large pile of pigeon poop. Unfortunately, Izzy didn't know about the pigeon poop until she used her left hand to push her hair out of her face, leaving a long, smelly white streak down her dark black hair. Izzy sat on the steps staring at her hand until she suddenly became aware of the sound of laughter. She looked up and saw three girls standing at the bottom of the stairs laughing hysterically.

"That was awesome!," howled the tall blond. "You are just soooo graceful." Her two friends nodded in agreement as they continued to laugh. "I just love what you did with your hair too. Those highlights look marvelous! Actually, the bird poop matches that ridiculous-looking hair band you're wearing. The feathers really bring out the bird poop. Smashing!"

Izzy self-consciously reached for her hair band. She had made it herself and it was her favorite. At least it had been her favorite.

The tall blond and her two side-kicks stood laughing at the bottom of the steps, each side-kick telling the tall blond how incredibly funny and clever she was. The blond-haired girl obviously enjoyed their adoration and praise and answered each compliment with a flamboyant toss of her hair and an arrogant "Oh please, you are really too kind."

To Izzy the tall blonde looked like a Barbie, a brand-new one right out of the box. She was tall and wispy thin with blue eyes, straight blonde hair, and a perfect figure. She was very tan, almost abnormally so, which made her white teeth seem even whiter and the bright red color of her lipstick was perfectly matched by the bright red color of her fingernails. Her shirt was from Abercrombie and Fitch, her jeans were

Calvin Klein, and her shoes were either Prada or Armani. Slung across her left shoulder was a black soft-leather Gucci purse which, of course, matched her belt and shoes.

"Sooo," the tall blonde said with more than a hint of self-importance, "we know you're quite clumsy and awkward. We know you have terrible taste in clothing, and we know you need a lot of help with your hair. What we don't know is your name." The side-kicks giggled in agreement as the blonde stood staring at Izzy.

"My name is Izzy Watson," she replied.

"Watson!," the blonde exclaimed. "Well, well. Girls, this is a member of the famous Watson family. They are practically royalty at Exeter." She looked accusingly at Izzy. "But surely you can't really be a Watson. They have all been intelligent, well-dressed, refined, talented, and pleasant. But you? You a Watson?" The blonde and her servants looked at each other with fake looks of shock on their faces and then burst out laughing.

Izzy had heard enough of this. The tall blonde was right about one thing. Izzy was different than the rest of the Watson family in one particular way. Izzy had a temper and Barbie had just lit Izzy's fuse.

She stood up and dropped the bag hanging from her neck. Before the giggling trio ever saw her she had a fist-full of the blonde-haired girl's expensive Abercrombie and Fitch shirt.

"Look Blondie, I've had enough of ......"

"Cassandra Smithton!," a voice called out. "What is the meaning of this?"

Izzy and the three other girls spun quickly around at the sound of the voice. A tall middle-aged man in a tweed jacket stood at the top of the steps. "Young lady," he said, "please release Miss Smithton."

Izzy reluctantly let loose and turned to face him as he slowly walked down the steps. Cassandra Smithton straightened her shirt as her two servants began to wildly explain to the man how Izzy had been rude to them and had attacked Cassandra.

"Enough!," the man said firmly. "That is a nice story but unfortunately for you I know that it is only a story. I heard everything that happened." He stretched out his arm and pointed at the building.

"You see," he said calmly, "my office is right there on the first floor and the window is open."

"But Mr. Crandall," Cassandra protested, "she …."

"I said that's enough Miss Smithton," Crandall said sternly. "The three of you should be ashamed of how you treated Miss Watson. I would expect better manners from you."

He turned and looked at Izzy. "And you Miss Watson. You must learn to control your temper, no matter what the provocation. There will be no fighting at Exeter Boarding School, ever, for any reason. Do you understand?"

"Yes sir," Izzy replied meekly.

"Now," Mr. Crandall said as he looked towards Cassandra and her friends, "you three go to your dorm rooms. Out of kindness I will not report this incident to the Principal. I would hate for your first day at Exeter to include a visit to Mrs. Thompkins office."

Cassandra and her two accomplices thanked Mr. Crandall for not reporting them, quickly ascended the steps, and disappeared through the door. Izzy walked slowly over to retrieve her suitcase and bag.

"Miss Watson," Mr. Crandall said, "may I have a word with you?"

"Yea," Izzy answered with a sigh of annoyance. She knew she was going to get a lecture and she absolutely hated to get lectured. She knew she was wrong, she knew she needed to learn to control her temper. What was there to talk about? Why did adults always feel like they need to tell you what you did wrong and then keep picking at it like a scab?

"I'm sorry you've had such a rough start here at Exeter," Mr. Crandall said. "But please don't let it upset you too much Isabella. Miss Smithton and her companions are a bit, shall we say "ill-mannered," but I believe you will come to like them in the end. And most of the students here are distinctly more courteous and more refined than those you have just met. So you needn't worry Miss Watson."

"Thank you," Izzy answered politely, relieved that she had avoided a lecture and grateful for Mr. Crandall's supportive words. "I should have behaved better but she really ticked me off. Next time I won't let her get to me."

"Very well, Miss Watson," Crandall replied. "Have a nice evening. You will find your room on the second floor, to the left down the hall." He turned and headed up the steps.

"Mr. Crandall?," Izzy called after him. "There's one more thing."

Crandall stopped and looked back at Izzy. "Yes, Miss Watson?"

"How do you know who I am," Izzy asked. "I don't think we've ever met."

"No, we have never been formally introduced," he replied. "I am Mr. Crandall, Roger Crandall. I will be your English instructor this year." He paused for a moment and looked directly into Izzy's eyes. "As to you're question Miss Watson, I know a great deal about you as well as a great deal about many other things. My sources for that information I shall keep to myself. I have high hopes for you at Exeter this year and I am confident that you will perform splendidly. Good day Miss Watson."

He turned quickly and walked through the door into Franklin Hall.

Izzy went over to a stone bench at the bottom of the steps and sat down. She reached into her shoulder bag, brought out a handkerchief, and wiped the pigeon crap off her hand and out of her hair.

Her wrist throbbed with pain from landing on it when she fell. It had really hurt when she grabbed Cassandra but she had been too angry to notice it. Now that the anger was gone the pain was back and Izzy could feel the swelling in her wrist as she gently rubbed it in a futile attempt to stop the pain. This certainly wasn't how she wanted her first day at Exeter to go. She had embarrassed herself, gotten in an argument with another student, and hurt her wrist. It was a disaster! What had Link said? Think positive?

"Link?"

"Yes Izzy," he replied.

"Did you see that?" Izzy asked.

"Of course I did," Link answered.

"I've only been here an hour and things are already a mess!," Izzy said excitedly. "Cassandra Smithton is a nightmare. I know it's wrong but I wish Mr. Crandall hadn't shown up so I could have smacked her a good one. Maybe that would teach her and her two giggle-buddies a lesson."

"I am certainly glad that Mr. Crandall was there to prevent such a thing," Link answered. "Violence will not solve the problem."

"I know, I know," Izzy said loudly. "Please no lectures now Link. Just let me vent. I can find another way of dealing with Cassandra Smithton besides beating her to a pulp. I've dealt with bullies before."

"Don't think about revenge Izzy," Link replied. "That doesn't work either."

Izzy dropped her head and slumped back on the bench. She knew Link was probably right. He always was.

"I'm sure you're right Link but that doesn't mean I have to like it," she said. "That girl is an arrogant snot and I'd love to put her in her place. But I won't. I guess I need to learn to "turn the other cheek" as they say.

"They do say that and I believe that would be the correct response," Link replied with a sense of relief.

Izzy paused for a moment and rubbed her wrist. "Forget about Cassandra," she said finally. "What do you think of Mr. Crandall?"

"He seems like a very nice, level-headed young man," Link answered.

"Yeah, he does seem nice," Izzy replied, "but don't you think its kind of strange that he knows so much about me?"

"I don't think it's strange at all," Link answered. "I'm sure he has talked with Principal Thompkins about you. After all, you are a Watson and the principal knows your family quite well."

"Yeah," Izzy answered, unconvinced. "Maybe you're right. It still seems a little weird though."

Izzy never heard the window open. They must have opened it when she was cleaning her hair. But now she heard the giggling. And then she heard the voice.

"Who are you talking to Watson?"

The sound of the voice startled her and her head whipped to the left. At first she didn't see anyone but then she looked up. Standing in an open second floor window was Cassandra Smithton with her two servants beside her.

Izzy glared at them. "Nobody," she answered.

"We heard you talking to somebody," Cassandra said. "Do you have a pet mouse or a hamster in your pocket?" Cassandra and the side-kicks erupted in laughter.

"It's none of your business," Izzy said coldly.

"Now Miss Watson, please try to control your temper," Cassandra said mockingly as her servants giggled. "I know! You have an imaginary friend. That's so cute!"

"He's not an imaginary friend!," Izzy shouted, unable to stop the words before they came out of her mouth.

Cassandra and her friends squealed with laughter. "So, you do have an imaginary friend!," Cassandra cried. "That's okay when you're six-years-old but its really pathetic when you're thirteen. Are you sure you're supposed to be starting the ninth-grade?"

"Shut-up Cassandra," Izzy replied angrily.

"I guess you need an imaginary friend when you don't have any real ones," Cassandra taunted.

"He's not an imaginary friend!" Izzy yelled, unable to control herself. "He's more like a guardian angel." Once again Izzy wished she had stopped the words before they left her mouth.

Cassandra and her friends exploded in a fit of laughter. "A guardian angel? That's a good one Watson," Cassandra snorted. "You really are a weirdo. There's no such thing as angels. Everybody knows that. Have you ever seen one?"

"No," Izzy answered softly, unable to mount any further defense.

"That's brilliant! You've never seen an angel but that doesn't stop you from talking to one," Cassandra said. "You really are weird. I think we'll just call you "Weirdo Watson." The servants howled with laughter as they gave Cassandra a high five. "Later Weirdo," she sneered as she slammed the window shut.

Izzy slumped against the back of the bench and stared at the ground. Her head was spinning.

Could this day get any worse? Her hair smelled like pigeon crap, her wrist was killing her, and she had just made a complete fool of herself. How could this happen? Why did she let Cassandra get to her like that? How could she have been so stupid as to tell them she had a guardian angel? She knew they would just laugh and make fun of her. The tears slowly ran down her face and Izzy could taste the salt in the corner of her mouth. Maybe they were right, she thought. Maybe she was weird, maybe she was too old to have an imaginary friend, a guardian angel. Izzy stood up and wiped the tears from her face.

"Link?"

"Yes Izzy," Link answered.

"I made a fool of myself," Izzy said as she struggled to hold back the tears. "They think I'm a total weirdo because I believe in angels."

"Weird?" Link replied. "What's weird about believing in something that is real?"

"I don't know what's real anymore," Izzy said quietly. "Everything used to make sense but now everything is so confusing. I find out I'm adopted. I'm at a boarding school that feels like a jail. And now everyone thinks I'm a weirdo. Everything is a mess!"

"It's been a tough day," Link said softly. "Things will get better."

"I don't know about that Link," Izzy sobbed, unable to hold back the tears any longer. "I don't know about anything anymore. And I don't know about you either! You got me into this. You said this was a great place and that there were a lot of nice people here. You were wrong. You lied to me! And then you made me look like a complete idiot!"

"Izzy..."

"You did! You did!," Izzy cried. "I never want to talk to you again!"

"Izzy, please, you're..."

"No, Link," Izzy yelled, "leave me alone. You're not even real. I never want to talk to you again!" Izzy grabbed her bags and ran up the steps into Franklin Hall.

A Little Help Never Hurts

Franklin Hall served as the dormitory for all of the female students at Exeter Boarding School. From the front it looked like a long rectangle but in fact it had a third wing sticking out behind so that it actually was shaped like an upside-down letter "T". Long corridors ran out in three directions from a large central atrium. The freshman, sophomore, and junior girls occupied separate wings of the second floor while the senior-class girls lived in the long central corridor on the first floor. The left-hand wing of the first floor was housing for the younger teachers and their offices were down the right-hand wing, separated by the open atrium and a large dining hall.

Franklin Hall had originally been the main schoolhouse. When new classrooms were built in Graham Hall the old classrooms in Franklin were divided by walls into three equal parts forming three long, skinny rooms each with a single window on the back wall. The walls were thick and high and the rooms had the look of a tall box. The ceiling and walls were covered with a dark wood paneling that was very shiny and smooth and each wall was outlined with ornately carved trim work at the top, bottom, and sides which made the wall look like a huge picture frame with no picture inside. The hardwood floors were a lighter color than the walls, especially near the doorway where countless footsteps had worn away the varnish and exposed the bare wood underneath.

Each dormitory room was furnished in exactly the same way as all the others. On the back wall were two twin beds, one on each side of the central window, covered by identical dark blue bedspreads. Along each of the two long walls were a four-drawer oak dresser, a large armoire, and a small desk with a lamp and chair. The only other furnishings were a large oriental rug in the center of the room and a coat rack near the door. Conspicuously absent was a bathroom. The bathroom and showers were located in the center of the long hallway, one on the right side and one on the left. No amount of begging or complaining by the students had ever convinced the Principal of Exeter Boarding School to construct private bathrooms.

Izzy's room was on the second floor, down the left hallway, at the end of the hall on the right. For some unknown reason she had not been assigned a roommate and thus she had the room to herself. For the first week or so it had bothered her not to have a roommate but she got over the initial loneliness and was happy to have her own room. What she wasn't happy about were the strict rules against rearranging furniture or decorating the room. All furniture was required to be left in place and nothing could be hung on the walls. Izzy was no delinquent and didn't mind following rules but after a few days she just couldn't take it anymore. The room had no color, no life, and she felt like she was living in a museum. She had to do something to give the room some character, some "Izzy-ness." But twice each week the school had mandatory room inspections and she couldn't always be taking things down and putting them up again.

There had to be a better way.

To solve the problem, Izzy pushed the two beds together in front of the window and turned them around so that the foot of the beds was against the bottom of the window. This allowed her to lean against the headboard and look out the window when she studied rather than having to sit at the cramped little desk where there was nothing to look at but the wall. To make the beds easier and quieter to move, and to avoid scratching the floor, she put socks on the bottom of the bed post so she could easily slide the beds back to their normal position.

She taped a long piece of string to the back of each headboard and hung colorful socks, hair-bands, and necklaces along the string. She cut pictures of various animals, a sunset, and a jungle out of some magazines and taped them to the back of the headboard. With the beds pushed together under the window the headboards added a lot of color to the room and when inspection day came Izzy simply pushed the beds back where they belonged, hiding the decorations against the wall. After three inspections Izzy noticed that the teacher never came into the room. She would simply stand in the doorway and briefly look around. So Izzy strung some beads across the back of the door and hung several dried flowers that she had picked from the garden behind Franklin Hall.

Two weeks into the school year Izzy was satisfied with her room but everything else was a complete mess. It had rained all day on the weekend and she'd had to spend all of her free time indoors. She had gotten a D on her first geometry quiz and a C minus on her English paper. To make matters worse, Cassandra Smithton was in her geometry class and her English class and had made a point of letting the whole class know Izzy's grade. Her left wrist was still swollen and painful and she had to sit and watch while the rest of the class played volleyball. But all of these other problems were minor in comparison to Izzy's main problem, the thing that bothered her the most. She couldn't talk to Link.

She tried every day, usually several times every day. But all she heard was silence. At first she thought that she had just hurt his feelings with the mean things she had said and that it would just take a while for him to get over it. She apologized several times; she had been angry and upset and hadn't meant what she said. The silence continued however and Izzy continued to fret. Maybe he was still mad?

But after two weeks of silence it was Izzy who was now mad. As she sat on her bed staring out the window thinking about Link she got even madder. She'd said she was sorry. What more did he want?

And where was he when she really needed him? All these problems and issues and he chooses now to run off and leave me? Fine! I don't need him anyway.

A sharp knock on the door jolted Izzy out of her thoughts. She glanced down at her watch. Seven- thirty on a Sunday night? Hopefully not a teacher. The beds were turned the wrong way and there wasn't time to put them back where they belonged.

"Who is it?" Izzy called as she jumped off the bed.

"Angela Wagner," a soft voice answered.

Angela Wagner? Who is Angela Wagner? Izzy didn't know but at least she knew there wasn't a teacher by that name at Exeter. She walked over and opened the door.

A short brown-haired girl in an Exeter uniform stood in the doorway. Actually, she was leaning in the doorway, her hand holding a thick wooden cane that caused her to tilt to the right. Around her right leg was a black metal brace that encircled her leg from just above the knee down to her heel and over the top of her shoe. She wore black tights under her plaid uniform skirt but they did not hide the fact that her right leg was much thinner than her left and also several inches shorter.

"Hello Isabella," she said. "I'm Angela Wagner."

"Hi Angela," Izzy answered, hopeful that Angela hadn't noticed her staring at her leg. "What can I do for you?"

"Well," Angela replied, "I guess I might as well just come out and say it. I'm your roommate."

"My what?" Izzy exclaimed. "My roommate? They said I didn't have a roommate."

"I guess they mistakenly thought that I wasn't coming to school," Angela said. "But I'm here and this is the only room available. I'm sorry to surprise you like this but Mr. Crandall said to come up here and he would bring the rest of my things tomorrow."

Izzy was confused and, though she was ashamed of herself for thinking it, annoyed. She had finally gotten her room how she liked it and had gotten used to having her privacy. Now her privacy was gone and she would probably have to put the room back like it was "supposed" to be. On top of all the other problems she had, now this!

"Okay," Izzy finally said, "come on in."

Angela shuffled into the room and set her backpack down on the floor next to the desk. She pulled the chair back from the desk, switched the cane to her left hand, grabbed the brace with her right hand, and swung her right leg forward while simultaneously dropping into the chair. She looked up at Izzy and smiled. "Cerebral palsy."

"Excuse me?" Izzy replied.

"My useless right leg is from cerebral palsy," Angela said calmly. "It's some kind of birth injury or something. I don't like it but I'm glad that's all that's wrong with me. Could be worse."

Izzy felt more than a little guilty. All of her problems seemed pretty small compared to this. "I'm sorry," Izzy said, not knowing what else to say and trying not to stare at Angela's outstretched leg.

"Don't be," Angela replied. "It certainly isn't your fault now is it? And I'm the one who should apologize. You looked like you had seen a ghost when you opened the door. I didn't mean to scare you."

Now Izzy really felt bad. Angela had obviously noticed Izzy staring at her leg! "I'm sorry Angela," Izzy stammered. "I, I was just surprised and ...."

"Don't worry about it Isabella," Angela answered with a smile. "I'm used to people staring at me. It doesn't bother me anymore. I'm different, so what? It's okay to be different."

Izzy smiled back at her. She smiled like she used to smile at home, like she hadn't done in the two weeks since she'd been at Exeter Boarding School. Here, finally, was something Izzy could understand. Different. It's okay to be different. TJISD.

"You're right Angela," Izzy said. "It is okay to be different."

"I knew you would understand," Angela answered happily. "I asked around about you when I heard you were going to be my roommate. They said you were different too. That made me feel better. And that other stuff, it doesn't bother me."

Izzy looked at Angela, her brief smile now completely gone. "What other stuff?' Izzy asked.

"Oh, nothing," Angela said sheepishly, looking quickly away towards the beds. "Oh, I really like what you've done with the room."

"Don't change the subject," Izzy said sternly. "What did you mean by "that other stuff"?"

Angela sighed and shifted in her seat. "That stuff with Cassandra Smithton on the first day of school. How a lot of people call you "Weirdo Watson." That doesn't bother me. People have always called me names and I know those names aren't true. So I know that "Weirdo Watson" isn't true either."

Izzy was quiet. She knew that a lot of the other kids called her "Weirdo Watson" behind her back. It bothered her a little but she was learning to ignore it. But having someone say it right to her hurt. She knew Angela didn't mean it but hearing the words still stung.

"Thanks for your support Angela but I don't need it," Izzy said sharply. "I don't care what they say about me. That's all in the past now and I'm moving on."

"Good for you Isabella!" Angela said. "It doesn't matter what they say. Who needs them anyway? You've got me and Mr. Crandall."

"Mr. Crandall?" Izzy replied, completely confused. "What does he have to do with any of this?"

Angela stared down at the floor. "Nothing."

"Come on Angela," Izzy said, "out with it. Friends don't keep secrets."

"Well," Angela said slowly, "when I heard about you and Cassandra I knew better than to believe it. I figured her story wasn't completely true. I've dealt with her type before. So I went and asked Mr. Crandall about it and he gave me the real story. We talked about it and we decided you were right."

Izzy was getting more confused. "I was right about what?" she asked.

"About guardian angels," Angela replied.

"Oh geez!" Izzy cried. "Not that again! I don't want to talk about it. I told you, its over, it's in the past."

"I don't think so," Angela said confidently.

"Please Angela," Izzy exclaimed, "that's enough. I'm through with all that. It was just a phase I was going through."

"A phase you were going through?" Angela asked skeptically. "Come on Isabella. I don't believe that and I don't think you do either. Don't tell me you believe Cassandra Smithton?"

"I don't know what to believe anymore," Izzy answered. "All I know is that I need to move on and try to somehow make it through my freshman year at Exeter. That's a big enough challenge without all this other stuff." Izzy walked slowly across the room and stood by the beds. "Now, I'm through talking about this. I'm tired and I'm going to bed. I'll push the beds back where they belong. I'll take the one on the left and you can have the one on the right."

Angela pushed herself up from her chair and stood looking at Izzy. "Wait a second," she said. "I like how you have them set up and I love the decorations. Can't we just leave them like they are?"

Izzy stared back at Angela. Despite the initial surprise and annoyance and despite the difficult conversation there was something about Angela that Izzy liked. She was smart, energetic, and confident and obviously didn't let her handicap get in the way. There was something else about her though, something that Izzy couldn't quite put her finger on. She was, well, Angela was just different.

Izzy smiled. "Sure Angela," she said. "You can have the one on the right. And, by the way, call me Izzy."

From Out Of The Blue

Izzy got up early the next morning before Angela or any of the other girls were awake. She didn't like the whole "bathroom scene" that occurred each morning before school. It was way too much drama for Izzy. Dozens of giggling teenage girls gossiped about this boy or that boy or about who liked who or about who was dating or who just broke up. Lines of girls formed in front of the mirrors as they frantically tried to make themselves prettier, covering their faces with eye shadow, eyeliner, foundation, lipstick, acne medicine and who knows what else. After that they all went to battle against their hair. They dried it, curled it, crimped it, braided it, and cursed it. Somehow in the midst of all this madness they still found time to talk about the other girls, about who was getting fat or who had a crush on a teacher or who colored their hair and all sorts of other back-stabbing and nonsense. The girls bathroom on the second floor of Franklin Hall was also where Cassandra Smithton held her royal court. Each morning her loyal subjects gathered around her so she could tell them what to think or give them beauty tips or use them to spread rumors. Often she simply stood in front of the mirror brushing her hair while her underlings told her how pretty or smart or popular she was, as if she didn't already know.

Izzy, of course, wanted no part of the bathroom scene. She had unknowingly gone there on the first day of school but had never gone back. Now she was in the shower by five-thirty every morning and safely back in her room by six, well before any of the other girls arrived on the scene. This gave her an hour to complete her homework or study for a test before she had to go down to breakfast at seven-fifteen.

This morning she had actually been a little late but she hurried through her shower and managed to escape before the other girls showed up. She walked quickly along the dim hallway, wondering whether Angela knew about the bathroom scene and reminding herself to warn her about it. Izzy came to her room and quietly opened the door so she wouldn't wake Angela. As she stepped into the room she heard a muffled crunching sound under her feet and looked down. In the faint light it was hard to see but it looked like she was standing on a piece of paper. Izzy bent down and picked it up. Rather than a piece of paper it was actually an envelope. She closed the door behind her, went over to her desk and turned on the lamp.

Izzy examined the envelope. It was small, the size a person would use to send out an invitation or a thank-you card. Though she had stepped on it the envelope wasn't crinkled or scuffed. She turned it over and across the front was written "Miss Isabella Watson" in a flowing black cursive. Izzy studied it for a moment and then tore it open, hopeful that perhaps a party invitation was inside. Maybe everyone at Exeter didn't think she was a weirdo. Inside the envelope was a piece of white paper neatly folded in thirds. Izzy unfolded the letter and read it.

See Not the Air That Gives You Breath
Yet Without It Certain Death
You Pass It By But Do Not See
Does That Mean It Cannot Be?
The Desert Boy He Sees Not Snow
Does That Mean No Blizzards Blow?
How Many Things The Hand Can't Feel
This Does Not Mean They Are Not Real
You Cannot See If You Close Your Eyes
Open Them If You Wish Be Wise

Izzy stared at the letter. She turned it over and looked at the back but it was blank. She read the letter again, slowly, struggling to figure out exactly what it meant. The desert boy he sees not snow? What in the world could that mean? She read it again, and then again, and as she did Izzy went from puzzled to alarmed. Yet without it certain death? That was too freaky. And the drawing at the bottom? It kind of looked like a spaceship but then again it looked more like an eye. Was someone watching her?

The door handle turned but Izzy didn't see it. Her back was turned towards the door and she was too fixated on the letter to notice. But she did hear the door open.

"Aaahh!," Izzy screamed.

The light flicked on as Izzy whirled towards the door. "Angela!" she yelled, her heart pounding so hard she could hear the "whoosh" in her ears, "what are you doing?"

"Doing?" Angela replied, her eyes wide. "I'm just walking into my room and you scream at me and then ask me what I'm doing?"

"I'm sorry Angela," Izzy answered breathlessly. "I thought you were still in bed."

Angela closed the door. "I went to take a shower," she said. "I heard you get up earlier so I figured I might as well get up too. It takes me a while to get ready since I have to gimp around with my cane. All the other girls came into the bathroom so I had to leave without putting on my make-up. I didn't think I looked so scary without my make-up that it would make you scream."

Izzy managed a laugh. "That's not it Angela," she said. "You look fine. You just startled me."

Angela shuffled over to her bed and sat down. "Startled you?" she said. "You couldn't hear me coming down the hall? I make enough noise with my brace and my cane on that stone floor to wake the dead!"

"No you don't either," Izzy laughed. "I was just pre-occupied."

"A love letter?," Angela asked with a coy smile.

"What?," Izzy answered.

"A love letter," Angela repeated. "Is that what has you pre-occupied?"

Izzy looked down at her hands. She had forgotten that she was still holding the letter. "This?," she said nervously as she quickly turned and stuffed the letter back in the envelope. "This is nothing. I was just thinking about my Geometry quiz."

"Geometry quizzes never make me scream," Angela said as she grinned at Izzy. "But if that's your story."

"It's not a love letter!" Izzy replied defensively. "I don't even like boys."

"Okay, okay," Angela laughed. "Don't get huffy. I was just teasing you."

Izzy sat down at her desk and began to pack her books and homework into her backpack. Her heart was no longer pounding but her head was spinning. She wanted to read the letter again but couldn't, not with Angela in the room. Izzy slipped the envelope into her backpack and closed the zipper. Maybe she would have a chance to look at it later. She swung the bag onto her shoulder and walked to the door. She opened the door half-way but then stopped and looked back. Angela was sitting on the edge of her bed with a small mirror putting on her make-up.

"Angela?," Izzy said, "which bathroom were you in this morning?"

Angela turned and looked at Izzy. "The one on the left," she said. "Why?"

"I was in the one on the left too," Izzy said. "I didn't see you in there."

"I must have gotten into the shower while you were still in your shower," she answered as she returned to putting on her make-up. "And I take a long time in the shower because of my leg. You must have gotten dressed and left before I was done."

"Maybe so," Izzy replied, trying to remember if she had heard a shower running while she was getting dressed. "I'm going to go down to breakfast. I need to get there early so I'll have time to study for geometry. I'll see you later."

"Bye!," Angela called as Izzy closed the door.

Izzy walked down the hallway, down the stairs, and into the dining room. The dining room was a huge circular room with high, vaulted ceilings and enormous windows that covered almost the entire north and south walls. It was one of Izzy's favorite places at Exeter but not because of the food, though the food was quite good. Izzy liked the dining room because it was open and bright and looked out onto the courtyard where she could see grass and flowers and trees. It was about the only place on campus where she didn't feel like she was in a box. She often came to the dining room to study after school rather than going to the library. The library was just another of the featureless rectangles at Exeter, a boring rectangular building with long rectangular shelves filled with rows of rectangular books. The dining room was round and bright and different and Izzy liked that.

She especially liked it today because it was nearly empty. As Izzy sat down at a table along the south window she could see only a few other students over near the north wall. She made sure they weren't watching and then carefully slid the envelope out of her backpack and pulled out the letter. It was written in a neat, flowing cursive but she couldn't tell whether it had been written by a girl or a boy. She studied the words, reading them over and over until she had all but memorized them. But she still had no idea what the words meant. Did they mean she needed to open her eyes and pay attention? Maybe her geometry teacher had written the letter in order to get her to pay attention in class. But what about Angela? It was very strange that Izzy hadn't seen her in the bathroom. Did she write it and slip it in under the door?

But, then again, maybe Angela was right and it was a love letter. Maybe some boy really did like her and wanted her to "open her eyes" and notice him. Maybe it was that tall blonde boy who had smiled at her the other day. But what about the drawing of the pyramid and the eye at the bottom of the page? What was that?

The more Izzy thought the more confused and frustrated she became. She had several theories about the letter but none of them really made any sense. She needed some help, needed someone who could explain the poem's meaning so that she could then figure out who had written it. But who? Link? No, he was no help anymore. She had always trusted him but now when she needed him he was gone. She would have to find someone else.

The eight o'clock school bell rang, jolting Izzy out of her thoughts. She had been so engrossed in the letter that she hadn't even eaten breakfast nor had she noticed that two other girls were now sitting at the table. She quickly folded the letter and stuffed it into her bag. For some reason the letter made her edgy and uneasy and she didn't want anyone to see it. If anyone saw her with a secret letter with a strange- looking eye on it they would just make fun of her. It would just give them another reason to call her "Weirdo Watson." And what if it was from a boy? If the other girls found out, if Cassandra Smithton found out, their teasing would be unmerciful. There was no way she was going to let that happen.

Izzy quickly left the dining room and headed for her class over in Graham Hall. As she walked along the sidewalk an idea suddenly popped into her head and she abruptly stopped. Yes, she thought, that would work. She went over to a stone bench, sat down, and pulled out the letter. She quickly copied the letter onto a piece of paper but left off the drawing of the pyramid and the eye. She put the letter back into her bag, placed the copy in her English notebook, and hurriedly made her way to Graham Hall.

The final class bell rang at eight-fifteen just as Izzy slipped into her English class. English had been one of her favorite classes in middle-school but this class was different. Middle-school English was about spelling and vocabulary but this class was more difficult. Here they learned about writing and comprehension and plot structure and symbolism. Their first assignment had been to figure out the meaning of a Shakespearean sonnet and Izzy had bombed. But what made the class even worse was the fact that Cassandra Smithton sat two desks behind Izzy and was not shy about raising her hand to answer a question so she could make sure that everyone knew how smart she was. Izzy could hear Cassandra giggle each time Izzy was called on and got the question wrong.

The only thing good about English class was that Mr. Crandall was the teacher. He was nice, never raised his voice, and was very funny. He acted out scenes from the books using different voices or funny accents and sometimes sang or dressed up as different characters. Mr. Crandall made English fun and the hour would usually fly by and be over too soon.

But today was different. Today the class seemed to drag on forever. Izzy checked the clock a dozen times but the hands seemed to be stuck in glue and barely moved. She fidgeted and shifted in her desk, hardly paying any attention to Mr. Crandall. He gave the students the last fifteen minutes of class to work on their assignment but when the bell finally rang Izzy's paper was blank. She sat at her desk until all of the students had filed out the door and then walked up to the teachers desk.

"Mr. Crandall," Izzy said, "could I talk to you for a minute?"

Mr. Crandall looked up and smiled. "Certainly Isabella. What can I do for you?"

"Well, um," Izzy stammered, suddenly uncertain. "I, I was reading a poetry book last night and I came across a poem that I can't quite figure out. I was hoping you could help me with it."

"I would be happy to try Miss Watson," he answered politely. "But a poem can mean different things to different people. Let me have a look at it. I shall give you my opinion, though of course that does not mean my opinion is correct or that yours is not."

Izzy pulled the copy of the letter out of her notebook and handed it to Mr. Crandall. He read it quickly and then stared up at the ceiling, deep in thought. He read it again and then slowly read it aloud. After another few moments of quiet thought he handed it back to Izzy.

"Very interesting!," Mr. Crandall said excitedly. "Very interesting indeed Isabella. Where did you find this?"

"Huh?," Izzy mumbled, not expecting the question.

"Where did you come across this poem?," he asked again. "Its quite intriguing. Do you know who wrote it?"

"No," Izzy replied nervously. "I found it in some poetry book in the library. I don't even remember which book it was. Do you know what it means?"

Mr. Crandall leaned back in his chair and twirled a pencil in his fingers. "I have my interpretation of the poem Miss Watson," he said, "but I should like to hear your's first."

Izzy was really getting nervous now. She just wanted the answer. Why couldn't he just tell her?

"Well," she said, "I guess it could mean to open your eyes so you can see things around you."

"Dig a little deeper Isabella," Crandall said. "I think there is more here than meets the eye, so to speak."

Izzy felt frozen. She swallowed hard and stared at the paper. "Maybe it means to open your eyes so that you can see things around you that you never knew were there."

"Bravo, Miss Watson!" Mr. Crandall replied. "I think you are getting closer to the truth, at least as far as the author of your poem is concerned. Perhaps it would help if I reminded you that great poetry, like great literature, often uses symbolism to make a point. The "eyes" in the poem may mean "to see" but what else might it mean to "open" them?"

Izzy was beginning to feel the way she usually felt in English class. Lost and confused. What do eyes symbolize? What else does it mean to open your eyes? She was starting to regret that she had opened her mouth and asked Mr. Crandall for help. But she had and now she needed to answer so he wouldn't think she was dumb or weird.

"I guess the "eyes" could also mean your heart and your mind. If you open your heart and your mind as well as your eyes then you could really "see." Just because the boy lives in the desert and has never seen snow doesn't mean snow doesn't exist. Things exist even if we haven't seen them."

"Well done Isabella!," Mr. Crandall exclaimed as he clapped his hands in applause. "You have found the deeper meaning of the poem. It says to open your heart and your mind to the many things in this world that you may not have seen but yet are very real. Just because one has not seen it or touched it does not mean it is not there. For many people "seeing is believing," but those with more wisdom know there are a great many things that you cannot see with your eyes that are as real as you and me. You just have to open your heart and your mind to "see" them."

Izzy smiled and put the poem into her backpack. "Thanks Mr. Crandall."

"You are most welcome," Mr. Crandall replied. "Thank you for sharing this wonderful poem with me.

And if you find out who wrote it please let me know. I would like to read more of this author's work."

"I will Mr. Crandall," Izzy said. "Thanks again."

Izzy hurried down the hall and headed for her next class though she knew there was no way she could pay attention to geometry. There are things out there that you can't see that are real? Mr. Crandall had answered some of the questions but a few of the biggest ones still remained. Who would send her a poem about real things that are unseen? And what about the pyramid and the eye? She hadn't been able to think of a way to ask Mr. Crandall about that without him wondering what this was all about. He would believe she was reading poetry but what would he think about a strange-looking pyramid and an eye?

Izzy was lost in her thoughts as she hurried down the hall and never saw the yellow "Caution-Wet floor" sign. She lost her balance as her left foot slid out from under her and her arms instinctively flew backward in a frantic attempt to grab something. Fortunately, her right hand managed to catch the top of an open locker door and she didn't fall though she did make a loud, hollow crashing sound as her head slammed against the locker.

"Are you okay?"

Izzy's hand was still clutching the locker while her legs were stretched out in front of her as if she were hanging from the door. She felt someone grab her by the arm and help her to her feet. She straightened herself and felt the back of her head where a large, painful knot had already formed.

When she looked up a tall brown-haired, brown-eyed boy was standing beside her and held her by the arm.

"Are you okay?" he asked.

"Yeah, I think so," Izzy answered. "My wrist and my head kind of hurt but I think I'm alright. Thanks for your help."

The tall boy smiled and let go of her arm. "No problem," he said. "You kind of have to help when a girl dives into your locker."

Izzy was so embarrassed she wanted to dive into the locker and shut the door. He was really cute and she had just made a complete fool of herself. "I'm so sorry," she said," I was thinking about something and not paying attention to where I was going."

"That's okay Isabella," the boy replied with a bright smile. "I don't mind you dropping in."

Izzy stared at him. "How do you know my name?" she asked. "Do we know each other?"

The boy's bright smile disappeared, replaced by a look of disappointment. "I thought we knew each other," he replied softly. "I'm in your English class and your geometry class. I'm Tom Andrews."

Izzy felt bad that she didn't know his name but she couldn't recall ever seeing him before. "Oh yea, of course," she said awkwardly. "I'm sorry. I'm just a little outta whack right now. I did just hit my head on your locker."

"Yea," he said, "are you sure you're okay?"

"I'm fine," Izzy answered. "My head hurts and I'm really embarrassed but I'm fine."

"You know Isabella…"

Izzy cut him off in mid-sentence. "Call me Izzy."

"Izzy?," Tom said.

"Yes, Izzy," she replied. "I prefer that to Isabella. All my friends call me Izzy."

A bright smile returned to Tom's face. "Alright," he said. "Izzy. That's a cool name. Anyway, I was wondering if you…"

The rest of the sentence was drowned out by the loud clang of a bell. Tom and Izzy looked at each other. They were late for class! Without a word they both turned and sprinted down the hallway, up the stairs, and then down another hallway toward the geometry room. As they got closer to the room they could see that the door was already closed which meant they would each get a demerit for being late.

Tom slowly opened the door and he and Izzy walked into the room, both out of breath from their run.

The teacher was standing at the blackboard in the front of the room as Tom and Izzy made their way to their desks. "Mr. Andrews! Miss Watson!," the teacher said loudly, "perhaps I should buy each of you a watch so that you can get to class on time."

"We're sorry ma'am," they answered simultaneously.

"I should hope so," the teacher replied. "Both of you will get a demerit for your tardiness."

The teacher turned and began writing on the board as Izzy slumped into her seat. She could hear the murmuring and the stifled giggles from the other students but she stared straight ahead as she got out her geometry book. A moment later she felt a tap on her shoulder but she knew better than to turn around. Cassandra Smithton sat at the desk directly behind her. Izzy ignored the tap on her shoulder but she couldn't ignore the whispered chanting that followed.

"Izzy's gotta boyfriend. Izzy's gotta boyfriend."

She turned around and gave Cassandra an angry look. But Cassandra Smithton wasn't afraid of an angry look. The chanting continued. "Izzy's gotta boyfriend. Izzy's gotta boyfriend.

Izzy spun around and glared at her. "Shut-up Cassandra!"

"Miss Watson!," the teacher exclaimed. "that is quite enough! First you are late and now you interrupt my class with a childish attack on Miss Smithton. You will pack up your things and report to Principal Thomkins's office immediately."

"But Miss Lewis!," Izzy protested.

"Enough Isabella!," Miss Lewis replied sharply. "Please do as you are told."

Izzy knew better than to argue with Miss Lewis. She quietly and quickly stuffed her book into her backpack and walked to the door. As she turned to close the door behind her she saw Cassandra give a slight wave while she silently mouthed "bye-bye."

Izzy closed the door and stood in the hallway, her jaw clenched and her face flushed red from anger and embarrassment. She was mad at herself for letting Cassandra get to her like that but mostly she was furious with Cassandra. What a witch! She had made fun of her, told everyone she was a weirdo, and now she had gotten her kicked out of class and sent to the Principal's office! Enough is enough. She'd had enough of Cassandra Smithton and was going to have to do something about it. Izzy wanted to walk back into the room and pull every hair out of her head but she knew she couldn't do that. Unfortunately, revenge would have to wait. She need to calm down and compose herself and think of what she could possibly say to Principal Thompkins.

Izzy need not have worried about what she would say to Principal Thompkins because she wasn't allowed to say anything. Students at Exeter Boarding School did not have a conversation with the Principal. The Principal talked and the student listened. Mrs. Thompkins had no interest in hearing any excuses nor in hearing the student's side of the story. In this particular case, as she made abundantly clear to Izzy, there was only one side to the story. Izzy was late, Izzy was disruptive, and Izzy was guilty. Case closed. Her actions were completely unacceptable and would not be tolerated at Exeter Boarding School. Principal Thompkins expressed dismay that a member of such a fine and distinguished family would behave in such an odious and distasteful manner. Out of respect for her mother she would not call her parents but any further problems would be dealt with most severely. Izzy's only words during her visit to Principal Thompkins' office were "Yes ma'am" when she was asked if she understood. She quietly got up off her chair and left the office, somewhat shaken but also relieved that things hadn't gone worse.

Izzy walked back to Graham Hall to finish the rest of the school day. Her punishment from Principal Thompkins was a week of "Room Arrest," which meant that for seven days she had to go to her dorm room immediately after school and could only leave her room to go to class, to the dining room, or to the bathroom. At the moment that didn't seem to be much of a punishment since that's what Izzy wanted to do anyway. She was upset and angry and she didn't want to talk to anyone and in fact went through the rest of the day without saying a single word to anyone. But Izzy didn't have to say anything. By lunch time the entire school knew what had happened, thanks of course to Cassandra Smithton. She had wasted no time in telling everyone how she had been attacked by the hysterical "Weirdo Watson" and that Izzy was now dating Tom Andrews, though she had no idea what Tom could possibly see in such a wild and unstable girl.

The day seemed to last forever but somehow Izzy managed to ignore the whispers and the stares from the other students and made it through the rest of the day. She immediately went back to her dorm room after school and stayed there all night. Angela brought her some food from the dining room and listened patiently as Izzy described her encounter with Tom Andrews, the fight with Cassandra, and her visit with Principal Thompkins. Angela was very supportive and understanding and after talking with her Izzy felt better, glad to have at least one friend at Exeter.

By nine o'clock Izzy was finished with her homework and went to bed. She was exhausted but a thousand thoughts whirled through her mind and frustrated her attempts at sleep. As she lay in bed uneasy and uncomfortable she thought about what Principal Thompkins had said, how she had wondered how a member of the famous Watson family could behave so badly. Because I'm not really a Watson, Izzy thought, I'm adopted. Maybe she should tell the Principal that so she wouldn't have to wonder anymore. But then Izzy started to wonder. If I'm not really a Watson then who am I? Am I more like my real parents, my birth parents, than I am my Watson parents?

Izzy suddenly remembered the letter. In the chaos and confusion she had forgotten all about it. What had Mr. Crandall said? There are things out there that you haven't seen but yet they are still very real? A strange thought slowly crept into Izzy's half-dreaming mind. Could that mean that her "real" parents were indeed real and were out there somewhere? Maybe they were trying to contact her? Maybe they wrote the letter?

Izzy turned and pulled the covers tightly over her head. That's crazy! How could they know I'm here and if they did know why wouldn't they just come and talk to me rather than writing some poem? It didn't make any sense. Someone else must have written it. Maybe it really was a love letter and Tom had written it. Or maybe Angela did and was trying to warn her about something. But what about the eye? Is someone, or something, watching me? What if that's the "evil eye"? The answers never came but the questions stopped as Izzy finally drifted off to sleep.

Man's Best Friend

Izzy had never really liked going to the zoo. She had gone dozens of times with her family or with friends or on field trips with her school but always after an hour or so she was ready to leave. It wasn't because she didn't like animals that Izzy didn't like going to the zoo. She loved all animals, except snakes and bats, and was crazy about dogs, cats, and birds. What bothered her was seeing the animals in cages, pacing anxiously or sleeping or sitting quietly with blank stares on their faces. When people complained that the animals weren't "doing anything" and called them lazy or boring or stupid, Izzy got mad. The animals weren't lazy or boring or stupid, they were sad! Izzy could feel it in her heart when she watched them. They needed room to move and something to do, a place that felt like home rather than a metal and cement box surrounded by steel bars or glass. They wanted to be free and the sadness in their eyes made Izzy sad too.

Izzy now felt like one of the animals at the zoo. A week of room arrest had meant a week of nothing but classes and sitting in her room. She was like a caged animal- sometimes she slept, sometimes she paced the floor, and sometimes she simply sat on her bed and stared out the window. Saturday had been the worst. Angela, who had been Izzy's only source of fun and conversation all week, had gone home for the weekend and Izzy was all alone. The weather was terrible. Rain all day long with a howling wind and temperatures in the thirties. Izzy spent most of the day staring out the window, feeling as bad on the inside as the weather was outside.

Sunday was her last day of room arrest but by now Izzy had had enough. There was no way she was going to spend another day trapped in her room. Life's too short for this she thought as she pulled on a pair of rubber boots. Luckily she still had her brother Charles' winter jacket and as she fastened the hood over her head she was sure no one would recognize her.

Izzy poked her head out the door and looked up and down the hallway. Nothing. She pulled the door shut behind her and quickly and quietly made her way down the hall. She stopped at the top of the staircase and peered through the railing down into the atrium on the first floor. Seeing no one around she hurried down the stairs and out the front door. It was still cold and windy but the rain had stopped overnight. Izzy pushed her hands deep in her pockets and headed down the sidewalk with no particular destination in mind.

The Exeter Boarding School campus was layed out in the shape of a large square, nearly a quarter of a mile long on each side. Fourteen buildings of different shapes and sizes were scattered about the campus, connected by long curving walkways lined with trees and gardens. The perimeter was enclosed by a wall which in most areas was made of stone but in other places was made of black wrought-iron or thick green hedges. Izzy wanted to avoid the sidewalks so that she wouldn't be seen and instead walked along the outer wall. It felt good to be outside. The air was cool and smelled strong and clean after the long rain. The leaves were changing color and the ground was littered with small piles of fallen leaves scattered about amongst newly-made puddles. Izzy wanted to run through the piles of leaves and stomp in the puddles but knew it was best not to draw attention to herself. It was enough just to be outside after a very long week.

She made her way slowly along the wall to the far corner of the campus behind the library. From here she could see the river through the bars of the wrought-iron fence and hear it as it flowed noisily over shallow rocks before it turned to the east and disappeared behind the hills. She turned to follow the fence but as she turned she noticed a path that came up the hill from the river and then stopped at the fence near where she was standing. It seemed odd that a path would stop at a fence. Izzy stepped back and looked at the fence. In front of her was a narrow gate topped by a wrought-iron arch wrapped in vines. At the center of the arch was an old, weathered sign with the letters "I H S." Izzy knew better, especially after this week, but her sense of curiosity was stronger than her sense of fear. She slowly looked left and right and then behind her back towards the school. She flipped open the latch, stepped through the gate, and gently closed it behind her.

The path turned to the left and then dropped down the hill. Izzy ran down the path so she could get out of sight of the school as quickly as possible and followed the path as it snaked its way through the woods towards the river. At the river the trail turned left and hugged the edge of the water as it headed upstream until after a few hundred yards it again turned into the woods. Izzy jogged along until she reached the top of a small hill where she stopped and lowered the hood of her jacket, warm and breathing heavily from the long run. She walked over to a fallen log and sat down. The air was wet and sweet and the sound of leaves rustling in the breeze was like music after a week stuck inside her room. Most of the trees were ash and walnut though there were a few large white oaks scattered about. The oaks were the music makers. They were always the last to shed their colors each fall and were still nearly covered with dry yellow-brown leaves.

Izzy leaned back against a rock and enjoyed the smell and the feel and the sound of the forest. But there was another sound. Izzy sat up and strained to hear it. There it was again, a short, deep booming noise. She stood up to look around but couldn't see anything. A few seconds later she heard the sound again, this time a little clearer and a little closer. Maybe it was a boat on the river or loggers or a plane? Again she heard it, louder. It was coming from the trail in front of her but Izzy couldn't see very far down the hill because of the trees. The sound came again and then again and by now she could hear muffled steps in the leaves. Now she was getting a little scared but her sense of fear quickly left her. It wasn't a plane or a boat! It was a barking dog!

Up the trail came a big yellow dog. When he reached the top of the hill he slowed to a walk and then came slowly over to

Izzy, sat down, and looked at her. Izzy could tell from his bark and from his eyes that he was a nice dog, a beautiful yellow Labrador Retriever. He was thin and muscular, with a broad head, short nose, and a brown leather collar around his neck.

"Well hello boy!," Izzy said as she reached down to pat his head. "What are you doing out here? Are you lost?"

The dog stared at Izzy and slowly wagged his tail from side to side in the leaves.

Izzy knelt down beside him and scratched him behind the ears. The collar didn't have any tags but there was a name stamped into the leather. Gabriel.

"Hello, Gabriel," she said. "I'm Izzy. Are you lost?"

Gabriel got up, walked to the edge of the hill, and looked down the path in the direction he had come from. Then he looked back at Izzy.

"Is that where your home is?," she asked.

Gabriel barked, walked over to Izzy, and pulled on the edge of her coat with his teeth.

Izzy laughed. "Okay, okay," she said, "I get your message. You want me to go with you. You sure are one smart dog. Let's go."

Gabriel started down the path with Izzy behind him. He didn't bark and walked slowly, pausing several times to make sure that Izzy was still following. They walked for about ten minutes as the trail wound through the woods and then crossed a small wooden bridge over a creek. After crossing the bridge Izzy noticed the smell of burning wood and looking up ahead she could see a small cabin with gray smoke floating above the stone chimney. Gabriel sat down at the beginning of a gravel path that led to the front porch of the cabin. Izzy came up beside him and stopped.

"Is this your home Gabriel?," she asked.

Gabriel barked his answer.

The cabin sat in a large clearing and was made of thick logs covered by a dark-green metal roof. A covered porch wrapped around the front and sides and a fenced garden sat beside the cabin while off to the left was a wood and stone barn with large white doors. It was an old place but everything was very neat and orderly and to Izzy it looked like a postcard, very peaceful and idyllic.

"You have a beautiful home Gabriel," Izzy said. "I assume that you don't live here alone."

Gabriel glanced quickly at Izzy and then started up the gravel path towards the house. Izzy followed him, still admiring the simple beauty of the place. He stopped at the bottom of the porch steps just as the front door swung open.

"Good afternoon Isabella."

The sound of the voice startled Izzy and she stopped in her tracks. A tall, slender older man stood in the doorway with a coffee mug in his hands. He was wearing jeans with a blue wool shirt, dark-brown work boots, and a tan ballcap. His hair was long and brown but was flecked here-and-there with gray and matched his well-trimmed beard. He had soft, friendly eyes separated by a strong, though somewhat short, nose.

"Hello," Izzy replied. "I'm sorry to bother you but I found your dog in the woods."

The man laughed softly. "I think it may be the other way around," he said. "I believe Gabriel found you in the woods."

Izzy smiled. “Yea, you’re probably right.”

“Either way,” the man said, “Gabriel and I are glad you stopped by. My name is Iam.”

“It’s nice to meet you,” Izzy replied. “You have a beautiful home. And I really like your dog.”

Iam closed the door to the house and walked across the porch. “Gabriel is a great help to me here Isabella. He’s very smart and dependable and he does a lot of very important work for me. Come, please sit down.”

He gestured toward the steps and Izzy sat down on the bottom step while Gabriel layed beside her in the grass.

Izzy looked up at Iam as she scratched Gabriel’s ears. “How do you know my name?”

“I know a lot of things Isabella,” he replied. “My eyes are always open.”

Iam’s answer puzzled her. “Really,” Izzy said, “how do you know my name?”

Iam laughed as he took a seat on the upper step. “Forgive me Isabella,” he chuckled. “I didn’t mean to be a smart-aleck. I work at Exeter. I’m the caretaker. I look after the grounds and care for the lawns and the flower beds and the hedges, that sort of thing.”

“Oh,” Izzy said, disappointed. Hearing the name of her school brought her rudely back to reality. She had been enjoying the woods so much she had forgotten all of the problems back at school. And now Iam had seen her. What if he told Principal Thompkins?

“By the way,” Iam said, “What are you doing out here in the woods? Are you lost or are you searching for something?”

"No, I'm not lost," Izzy said. "I was out for a walk, getting some fresh air, and I saw the gate and just decided to follow the path."

Iam smiled. "You came through the narrow gate?," he said. "Very good. Not many people come through the gate to find me. But Gabriel and I are certainly glad that you did."

"I'm glad too," Izzy said. She stood up and looked around the clearing. "This place is awesome! It's so pretty and quiet and peaceful. It's a lot better than where I've been the last few days."

"Yes," he said, "you've had a very rough week."

Izzy turned and stared at Iam. "How do you know that?"

Iam took a drink from his cup and set it down next to him. "I already told you," he answered. "And I know Cassandra, though she doesn't know me very well."

Izzy's teeth clenched at the sound of Cassandra's name. Hearing that name ruined the fun of being in the woods.

"Iam? That's a different name," Izzy said as she tried to change the subject. "I've heard the name "Ian" but never "Iam." Is that Irish or something?"

"I guess you could say it's a family name," Iam answered. "It's quite unique. I believe I am the only Iam."

"Probably so," Izzy replied. "You're the only one I've ever met."

Iam stood up, walked down the steps, and looked up at the sky. "It's getting late Isabella and the wind has shifted directions. It might start raining again. I think you had better get started on your way back to Exeter or you'll get caught in the rain. Let me grab my coat and I'll walk you back."

"That's okay Iam," Izzy said confidently. "I can find my way back. I've spent a lot of time in the woods."

"Okay," Iam said reluctantly. "If you say so. But at least take Gabriel with you. If he's with you I know I won't need to worry."

"Great!," Izzy said. "I love dogs and I've missed not having one around." Izzy turned to go down the gravel path but then stopped. "You know Iam," she said, "could I ask you a favor?"

"Of course Isabella," Iam replied.

"Well," Izzy started. "do you think there's any way I could come back out here? I mean, I just love it here. It's so beautiful and you have a dog. Maybe I could do some work for you. I don't want to bug you or anything but I really would like to come back."

Iam looked down at Izzy and slowly scratched his beard. "I don't know Isabella," he said. "Wouldn't you rather spend time with your school friends? It's just Gabriel and I out here and you'd probably be bored." He stopped and his face broke into a bright smile. "I would think that you and your new friend Tom Andrews would be spending a lot of time together."

"Very funny!," Izzy said sternly. "I guess Cassandra told you about my "boyfriend." Well, for your information, he's not my boyfriend and….."

"Easy Isabella!," Iam laughed. "I was just teasing you. I'm sorry. I forgot about your temper. I just thought you'd rather spend time with your friends than out here in the woods with me and Gabriel. But have it your way. We would love to have you. There's lots of work to do to get ready for winter. You will work, won't you?"

"You bet I will," Izzy answered enthusiastically. "I'll work really hard. And if I start to bug you, you can just tell me to leave."

"I doubt that will be necessary," Iam replied. "Now get going. And take Gabriel with you."

"Thanks Iam," Izzy said. "This has been a great day. You've given me hope that I can make it through the school year."

"You are most welcome, Isabella," he said. "And I won't say anything."

Izzy looked at Iam, puzzled by his comment. "Say anything?," she asked. "Say anything to whom?"

"To Principal Thompkins," he replied. "About you being here today. But only this one time Isabella. You need to follow the rules."

Izzy grinned. "I will," she said. "Thanks Iam. C'mon Gabriel."

Izzy turned and ran down the path with Gabriel bouncing along beside her. She ran half-way back to the gate, stopping at the river to pick up a stick for Gabriel to fetch. He was a great retriever and never lost the stick and always brought it straight back for Izzy to throw again. She threw it over and over until they reached the bottom of the hill near the fence. Gabriel dropped the stick at the foot of the hill and sat down on the path looking up towards the gate. Izzy picked up the stick and tossed it up the hill but Gabriel didn't move.

Izzy reached down and patted his head. "I guess you're not supposed to go near the gate, huh?" she said.

Gabriel didn't move and looked up at Izzy. She knelt down and hugged him. "You're a great dog," she said. "Thanks for coming with me. I can get home from here. Go home now. Hopefully I'll see you soon."

Gabriel stood up, turned around, and slowly jogged back down the trail.

Izzy walked up the hill to the gate and peered through the bars to make sure no one was watching. She opened the gate, stepped through, and turned around to shut it. She glanced up at the arch and the wooden sign. I H S. The "I" obviously stood for "Iam" but what did the other letters stand for? She'd have to remember to ask him the next time she saw him. She turned around and hurried down the fence toward her dorm room as a light, cold rain began to fall.

Izzy walked into Franklin Hall and saw a few older students sitting in the dining room but nobody noticed her. She made her way up the stairs and turned down the hall towards her room. Suddenly, Izzy froze. Principal Thompkins! The Principal walked to the end of the hall and stopped in front of the door to Izzy's room. As Izzy stood frozen in the hallway Mrs. Thompkins stretched out her hand and knocked on the door. Oh no! Izzy's heart pounded. If she was caught out of her room she would probably get another week of Room Arrest, or worse. The Principal reached out and knocked on the door again. This time the door opened.

"Good evening," Principal Thompkins said. "I would like to speak to Miss Watson."

Izzy's heart sank. She'd had it now!

"Good evening Principal Thompkins," Angela replied calmly. "I believe Miss Watson is down the hall in the girl's restroom."

Izzy immediately ducked into the girls' bathroom. She frantically pulled off her rubber boots and her coat and hid them in the shower. She quickly stripped off her clothes and wrapped a towel around her body and another around her head.

"Miss Watson?"

Izzy turned and saw Principal Thompkins as she walked into the bathroom.

"Yes ma'am," Izzy replied.

"Sit down Miss Watson," the Principal said sternly.

Izzy slumped into a chair along the wall, certain that she'd been caught.

"I would hope that you have learned your lesson after your week of Room Arrest," she said. "Would I be correct?

"Yes ma'am," Izzy answered.

"Very well then," the Principal said. "I will officially release you from your punishment. But please be aware that any further foolishness will be dealt with in the harshest of ways. Do we understand one another?"

"Yes, ma'am," Izzy answered.

"Splendid," Principal Thompkins replied. "Good night Isabella."

"Good night ma'am," Izzy said.

Principal Thompkins turned and walked noisily out of the bathroom. Izzy sat motionless, hardly breathing, as she listened to the footsteps disappear down the hall. When she could no longer hear them she threw back her head and let out a deep breath. That was close, way too close. She hurriedly grabbed her boots and coat, picked up her clothes, and ran down the hall to her room. She flung the door open, dropped everything she was carrying, and threw herself at Angela.

"Thank you. Thank you, thank you!," she cried as she wrapped her arms around Angela, nearly squeezing the breath out of her.

"Easy Izzy!," Angela cried, "I break easy."

Izzy laughed and released her. "You're awesome! You should be an actress," Izzy said excitedly. "That was brilliant. "I believe Miss Watson is in the girls' restroom." Absolutely brilliant!"

"Well thank you Izzy," Angela replied as she pushed Izzy away from her. "I'm glad my brilliance could cover for your insanity. What were you thinking? Where have you been? I've been here for three hours. I assume you haven't been in the bathroom that long?"

Izzy laughed and reached out to ruffle Angela's hair. "Of course not silly!" she said. "I went for a walk."

"Where to?," Angela exclaimed. "Texas?"

"No, not to Texas," Izzy replied with a laugh. "I was in the woods. It's a long story. But right now I'm freezing cold and I'm starving. I haven't eaten all day. I need to take a hot shower and get something to eat. After I get cleaned up do you want to go downstairs and eat and I'll tell you all about it?"

"No thanks," Angela said. "I already ate and I need to finish my essay for English class tomorrow. Go do your thing and you can tell me all about it when you get back."

Izzy grabbed some clean clothes and her shower bag and went back to the bathroom. She took a long, hot shower, dried her hair, and got dressed. By the time she got downstairs the dinner hour was over and she had to settle for a cold sandwich and a candy bar from the machine though as hungry as she was she was happy to eat anything. When she got back to her room Angela was already asleep, her English note- book lying open on the bed beside her. Izzy put on her pajamas and crawled into her bed with her American History book. Somehow she managed to study for almost an hour though it was hard to concentrate. So much had happened today and her mind kept wandering back to the woods.

Angela moaned in her sleep and rolled over in bed. Izzy closed her book and looked at Angela. What a great roommate. Without her the last week would have been unbearable and she would have been completely busted by Principal Thompkins. Izzy slid off the bed, walked over to her desk, and pulled open the drawer. She needed to do something for Angela, something nice to thank her for everything she had done. She took a large black hair clip out of her drawer and laid it on the desk. For the next hour Izzy worked on the hair clip, wrapping the edges with tan leather and the teeth with alternating blue and yellow thread.

She glued rhinestones on the leather and hung four small white feathers off each side. Izzy held the hair clip out in front of her, turning it left and right as she admired it. It would look perfect on Angela. She placed the hair clip on Angela's desk, turned off the light, and went to bed.

A Bad Hair Day

Monday mornings can often be painful and unpleasant. After the fun and relaxation of the weekend it's hard to go back to the work and grind of a school day. Everybody's favorite morning is a Saturday or Sunday; no one would ever pick Monday. But this particular Monday morning was different, at least for Izzy Watson. She was relaxed and happy and more than ready to start a new day. She'd had a great weekend, her first great weekend since she had come to Exeter Boarding School, and it carried over into Monday. She had survived a week of Room Arrest, had a great friend in Angela, and had something to look forward to with the farm and Iam and Gabriel. In short, Izzy now had hope, hope that she had at last turned the corner and could make it through her freshman year. She wasn't about to let a little thing like a Monday morning get in her way.

And the morning started wonderfully. Angela absolutely loved her new hair clip. When she saw it laying on her desk she at first thought it was Izzy's. Izzy told her it was her gift, a gift for being such a good friend, and Angela nearly broke down and cried. The two friends laughed and hugged and talked for almost an hour and nearly made themselves late for class. Izzy slipped through the door into her English class just as the final bell sounded.

Today was the first day for students to give their oral reports. Each student was required to write a three page essay and then give a presentation in front of the class. Fortunately for Izzy, who absolutely hated public speaking, the teacher decided to have the students go in alphabetical order. With her last name being "Watson" she wouldn't have to do her presentation until Wednesday and so today she could just sit at her desk and relax. But what was good for Izzy was bad for Tom Andrews. The "A" in his last name meant that he would have to go first. As Tom anxiously walked to the front of the class Izzy could see Cassandra Smithton out of the corner of her eye. She turned away but could hear Cassandra's whispered chant- "Izzy's gotta boyfriend. Izzy's gotta boyfriend."

Tom started his presentation by writing a brief outline of his talk on the board. The title was "Tsunami- Out of Nowhere," and when he finished the outline he walked over to the wooden podium and began his talk. He seemed nervous and talked too fast as he hurried through his notes without ever looking up at the class. Izzy felt sorry for him. She knew what it was like to stand up in front of people, terrified and feeling the piercing stares of the audience. But she thought he was doing pretty well and only hoped that when it was her turn she wouldn't totally embarrass herself in front of Tom and Cassandra Smithton. Though the delivery was bad Tom's talk was very interesting and told the story of the recent Christmas Day tsunami that hit Indonesia and included an elaborate diagram showing how the waves spread outward from the center of the earthquake for hundreds of miles.

"So," Tom said, "in conclusion, that is the story of the great Indonesian Tsunami. I think it is very interesting, and a little scary, that there are things out there that you can't see or feel that can kill you. The earthquake that caused the tsunami was too far away for most of the victims to feel and they never saw the waves until it was too late. Most of the people had never even heard of a tsunami. But unfortunately, just because you can't feel it or see it doesn't mean that it's not real. Thank you." Tom gathered his papers off the podium and headed to his desk as the class politely applauded.

Izzy sat frozen at her desk, her eyes wide and mouth open as her mind struggled to understand what she had just heard. What was it Mr. Crandall had said about the strange poem she had received? Hadn't he said it meant that there were things out there that you couldn't see or feel but yet they were very real? And now Tom Andrews had just said the same thing! Izzy leaned forward and stared at the chalkboard.

Tom's outline was written in cursive, a compact and neat cursive with flowing letters. Izzy swallowed hard to try to get rid of the lump in her throat. Tom's writing looked a lot like the writing on her letter! Or did it?

"Isabella!"

Izzy nearly jumped out of her desk. Shocked back to reality she could now hear the rest of the class laughing and looked up to see Mr. Crandall standing next to her. "Yes Mr. Crandall," she stuttered.

"Mr. Andrews certainly gave a nice presentation Isabella but I didn't think that it would leave you speechless," he said as the class exploded in laughter. "Perhaps now you could answer the question that I have already asked you twice."

Izzy squirmed in her chair. "What was the question again?," she asked quietly as the class continued to snicker at her discomfort.

"Never mind Isabella," Mr. Crandall replied as he walked over to his desk. "Perhaps someone else can answer the question for me?"

Izzy shrunk down in her chair. She was embarrassed and humiliated and it didn't make her feel any better to hear Cassandra Smithton answer the question correctly or to hear Mr. Crandall praise her for her "astute and quite clever response." She wanted to throw up. Now she was not only embarrassed, she was mad. She'd made a fool of herself again and Cassandra had come out looking all smart and perfect, as usual. Izzy sat slumped in her desk for the rest of the hour, fuming and barely paying attention to the rest of the presentations.

Finally, the school bell rang and Izzy sat up in her chair as the other students slowly filed out of the room. She turned to grab her sweater off the back of her chair and when she turned back around she was startled, and annoyed, to find Cassandra Smithton and two of her friends standing beside the desk.

"You were awesome Watson!," Cassandra said with a smirk as her two friends giggled behind her.

"Were you in some kind of trance or something? No, that's not it, is it? Actually, you were so amazed at how gorgeous Tom Andrews is that you couldn't speak!."

Izzy's fist began to clench as she rose up out of her chair. "Shut-up Cassandra."

Izzy felt a pull on her arm and she instantly spun around and grabbed at the hand that held her.

"Whoa Izzy!," Tom said, releasing Izzy's arm. "I just wanted to talk to you."

Cassandra and her two puppet-friends laughed and walked away. Izzy stood glaring at them until they disappeared out the door.

"Why didn't you let me punch her a good one?," Izzy said as she turned back to Tom.

"That'll only hurt you Izzy, not Cassandra," Tom replied.

"I don't know about that," Izzy huffed, her hand still clenched into a fist. "I think it would feel good to bop her a good one right in her pretty little nose."

"Relax Izzy," Tom said. "Don't pay any attention to her. She's rude to everybody so don't take it personally. I don't. She's just a bad smell."

"A what?," Izzy asked. "Cassandra's a bad smell?"

Tom laughed, reached down, and opened Izzy's fist. "Yea, Cassandra's a bad smell," he said. "It stinks and it's annoying but it can't hurt you."

Izzy relaxed and managed a weak smile. "I certainly never thought of Cassandra Smithton as a foul odor but I sure like the idea," she said.

"Now that's better," Tom said, "I like you a lot more when you smile."

Izzy's smile brightened and she looked into Tom's eyes but then quickly turned away, feeling awkward and a bit flustered as she fumbled with her backpack and tried to think of something to say.

"I liked your talk," she said nervously, "it was very interesting."

"Thanks," Tom said. "I can't stand public speaking. It doesn't even matter how I did. I'm just glad it's over."

"You did great," Izzy replied. "It was really interesting. In fact, I want to learn more about it. You talked a little fast and I missed a few things. Could you write down some of the words, like tsunami or some of the names of the places where it happened. I'd like to check it out on the internet and read more about it."

Tom gave her a doubting, dubious look. "You're kidding, right?"

"No, really," Izzy said, "I want to look it up."

She handed Tom her notebook and a pen and he jotted down a few words. As he handed the notebook back to her the class bell rang.

"Not again!," Izzy cried.

"Bye Izzy," Tom answered as he bolted out the door.

There was no way she was going to run into Geometry class with Tom Andrews again. She wouldn't give Cassandra any more ammunition. She still had two minutes before the tardy bell rang so she slipped her notebook into her backpack and walked down the hall. She turned up the stairs and then down the hall and reached the door to the class as the second bell rang. Luckily, the teacher was talking to another student and had her back turned as Izzy quietly slipped into her seat.

It didn't take very long. "Izzy's gotta boyfriend. Izzy's gotta boyfriend," Cassandra whispered behind her.

Izzy tightened in her seat but didn't move. She felt a tap on her shoulder and heard another chorus from Cassandra but again Izzy ignored it. She felt the urge to turn around and slap Cassandra across the face but the temptation quickly faded. It was replaced by an overwhelming urge to laugh as Izzy thought about what Tom had said. She's just a bad smell. Annoying but harmless. She had to cover her mouth to keep from laughing out loud.

Izzy usually found Geometry class boring but today it bordered on unbearable. It dragged on and on and on and she couldn't focus on geometry because her mind was still on her English class and Tom Andrews' presentation. She couldn't believe he had said exactly the same thing in his talk as was written in her letter. Angela must have been right and it was a love letter. And Tom had written it! But maybe it was just some kind of strange coincidence. She wasn't sure and she couldn't exactly just come out and ask him if he wrote it. If he didn't write it she would look like a complete weirdo. The only way to know was to compare the writing she had gotten from Tom to the writing on the letter and see if they matched. She couldn't wait for Geometry class to get over!

But the detective work would have to wait. For now, Izzy was stuck in Geometry class. To make matters worse the teacher was walking around the room handing out the quiz, a quiz Izzy had completely forgotten about until it landed on the desk in front of her. Izzy stared blankly at the first page, her mind so scrambled she hardly even recognized any of the problems or formulas. It was as if the quiz was written in Chinese or Egyptian. Ten minutes later she had completed only one of the twelve problems on the first page and there were eight more problems on the second page.

Izzy looked over at the clock. Twenty minutes left to finish nineteen Geometry problems. She leaned back in her chair and closed her eyes tightly as if she were trying to squeeze all the other thoughts out of her head. "Focus," she said softly, "you gotta focus." She took a long deep breath and then nearly attacked the quiz, finishing four problems in seven minutes. She tore through five more problems and turned to the second page as she glanced at the clock. Seven minutes left. She clenched her jaw and scribbled furiously until the teacher called out "Time!." The last four problems on the sheet were completely blank.

The other students headed for the teacher's desk to hand-in their quiz as the bell rang. Izzy sat at her desk, disappointed and certain that she had failed, as the rest of the class filtered out of the room. Finally, she stood up, walked across the room, and dropped her quiz on the pile.

Miss Lewis looked up from her desk. "Is something wrong Miss Watson?"

"No ma'am," Izzy answered as she headed for the door.

"Miss Watson," the teacher called-out. "One moment please."

Izzy stopped and turned around. "Yes ma'am?"

"What is that in your hair?," Miss Lewis asked as she stood up from her chair.

"In my hair?," Izzy asked. "There's nothing in my hair."

"There is Isabella," Miss Lewis replied, "in back, near your shoulder."

Izzy twisted her head and reached back to feel her hair. She grabbed a few times until her hand landed on something soft and sticky. She pulled her long black hair over her shoulder so she could see and suddenly her face turned bright red. Cassandra!

"Oh my, Miss Watson!," the teacher exclaimed. "You have a large piece of gum stuck in your hair. Oh mercy! It's hopelessly stuck and matted Isabella. I'm afraid you might have to cut your hair in order to get it out! How in the world did you get gum in your hair?" Izzy was so mad she couldn't speak. How? How did I get gum in my hair? Cassandra put it there when she tapped me on the shoulder, that's how! She thought about telling Miss Lewis but knew it wouldn't help. Cassandra would just deny it.

"I have no idea," Izzy answered softly, struggling to control her anger. "Miss Lewis, would you please give me a pass so I can go to my room and take care of this? I can't go to my next class with a big wad of gum in my hair."

"Oh yes, child, of course," she answered as she scurried over to her desk. "I'm so sorry Isabella. You have such beautiful hair too. What a shame." She quickly wrote out the pass and handed it to Izzy. "Here now," she said, "go on back to your room. I will let your teacher know that you won't be to class today. I'm so sorry Miss Watson."

Izzy thanked her and walked out into the hallway. She wanted to cry but there was no way she was going to let Cassandra Smithton make her cry. If anyone was going to cry it would be Cassandra, not her. She threw open the doors and stepped outside, her mind busy with thoughts of revenge as she hurried down the sidewalk towards Franklin Hall.

"Where's the fire Isabella?"

Izzy stopped and turned towards the voice. Iam stood in the middle of a flower garden as he casually leaned on a rake, his hat in his hand and a broad smile on his face. "You really seem to be in a hurry," he said. "Are you on your way to a fire?"

Izzy managed a weak smile. "Hi Iam," she answered. "I'm sorry. I didn't see you there. How are you?"

"I am fine," Iam replied. "I'm sorry to see that you are not so fine."

"Yea, well, it's a long story," Izzy said.

"Indeed," Iam said casually, "it is a long story and a very old one too. But it won't work Isabella."

Izzy stared at him, confused. "What won't work?"

"Revenge," he answered.

"But she started it!," Izzy cried. "I've never done anything to Cassandra and all she's ever done is torment me. She makes fun of me, she laughs at me, she tries to embarrass me. And now this! Look at my hair!" Izzy grabbed her hair and thrust it out for Iam to see.

"I know you're angry Isabella," Iam said calmly. "Cassandra is wrong to treat you the way she does. But doing something back to her won't make it any better. It will just make matters worse."

Izzy was getting mad. It seemed like Iam was taking Cassandra's side. "Maybe it will, maybe it won't," she answered tensely. "I don't really care. I've had enough of Cassandra Smithton! It's like they say- "An eye for an eye."

Iam looked at Izzy, his smile now replaced by a sober look of concern. "But they also say "Turn the other cheek," he replied.

Izzy stood quietly for a moment as she thought about what Iam said. "I don't know if I can do that," she answered. "She's impossible! I wish she would just go away and leave me alone."

Iam laid down his rake and pulled off his work gloves. "Getting rid of Cassandra won't solve the problem either," he said.

"Yes it will," Izzy protested. "No Cassandra, no problems."

"It's not that easy Isabella," Iam replied. "It might solve this particular problem but another one will pop up to take its' place. You're always going to have problems to deal with. It's important to learn how to deal with problems rather than just wishing they would go away."

Izzy was getting mad again. She knew he was right but it hardly made her feel better. Iam was nice and he spoke softly but he was still giving her a lecture and she hated lectures, especially one telling her to be nice to Cassandra Smithton. "I'm sure you're right Iam," Izzy said defiantly. "I doubt I could be lucky enough to have Cassandra just disappear. I'll have to find some other way to deal with her because she's making my life miserable."

Iam looked at Izzy for a moment then slipped on his gloves, picked up the rake, and went back to working the ground. "Just remember Isabella," he said without looking up from his work, "no one can "make" you anything. You control how you feel and how you act. Happiness comes from the inside Isabella, not from the outside."

Izzy was irritated and had heard enough. She didn't need catching little slogans to help her deal with Cassandra Smithton. She already had a few good ideas of how to do it. "I've got to get going," she said. "I'll see you later."

Iam didn't look up and kept raking the dirt. "Goodbye Isabella."

Izzy turned away and headed down the sidewalk toward Franklin Hall. As she neared the bottom of the steps a thought suddenly occurred to her. She quickly stopped and turned to look but Iam was already gone. Izzy stood at the bottom of the steps, confused and nearly shaking. How did he know? She hadn't said anything about what had happened with Cassandra but somehow he seemed to know all about it. He had even known she was thinking about how to get back at her and told her it wouldn't work before she ever mentioned it! Izzy sat on the step as she searched for some reasonable, logical explanation. She struggled to push the weird, even creepy, thoughts out of her head. It was as if Cassandra Smithton was literally driving her insane, making her think crazy, wild thoughts about Iam and mind-reading and spies. Luckily, after a few anxious moments, a perfectly reasonable and logical explanation occurred to her. Iam had obviously heard Cassandra bragging to her friends about what she had done. After class she had probably gone outside and told her two side-kicks about it. Izzy could see them in her mind, laughing and giggling as they praised Cassandra for her evil genius. No doubt Iam had seen all this and just naturally assumed that Izzy would want revenge. Who wouldn't?

Izzy got up and walked up the steps into Franklin Hall. She showed her pass to a teacher in the atrium and went up the stairs and into the bathroom. As she walked into the bathroom she pulled the scissors out of her backpack, laid the backpack on a bench, and then stood in front of the mirror. Don't think about it. Just do it. Izzy swung her hair over her shoulder and grabbed it with her left hand. Calmly, she reached up with the scissors, cut off a six-inch piece of her long black hair, and dropped it in the trash can. Again, and then again, she cut until her hair was even and the trash can was nearly full. She brushed her hair, pulled it back into a ponytail, and walked out of the bathroom.

Izzy turned left down the hallway and walked toward her dorm room. Because of Angela's excitement over the hair-clip this morning she had missed breakfast and had forgotten her lunch pass. She was starving and needed to go to her room to get the pass before lunch. She pushed open the door, stepped into the room, and turned to close the door. Instantly, her heart jumped and her hand flew up to her mouth to cover her scream. It can't be! Lying on the wooden floor inside the door was a small white envelope.

Izzy stared at the envelope as if it were a snake, not sure whether she should stand still or run. Slowly and carefully she bent down and picked it up as she pushed the door closed. It looked just like the first envelope she had gotten, clean and white with large, black cursive letters reading "Miss Isabella Watson."

Izzy sat down at her desk, flipped on the lamp, and opened the envelope.

The Age-Old Battle Rages On
The Evil One Is Never Gone
A Roaring Lion Is On The Prowl
Do Not Run When You Hear His Growl
Stand Tall Upon The Primal Stone
Remember That You Are Not Alone
Use The Strength That Lasts Forever
The Hands Have Power When Put Together
The Old Ones Speak An Ancient Tongue
Use Their Words To Fight This One

Izzy sat at the desk for several minutes, hardly breathing as she read the letter over and over and stared at the hand. The meaning of the letter was beyond her but the feel of it was not. It seemed different from the first one, comforting rather than spooky, even though she had no idea what it really meant. She pulled the first envelope out of her backpack and laid the two letters beside each other. The paper and the writing were identical. She pulled her notebook out of the bag and opened it to the page that Tom Andrews' had written on. The writing was similar but it was hard to be sure if it was the same. But if it wasn't Tom Andrews than who was writing the letters? Angela? Maybe but that didn't make any sense. For a brief moment Izzy thought of Link but quickly pushed the thought out of her mind. Cassandra and these letters are making you crazy she said to herself.

Izzy glanced at her watch. Ten twenty-five. Her pass was only good for an hour and she had to be in History class in five minutes. Reluctantly, she folded the letters, stuffed them in the envelopes, and put them in the desk drawer. It would have to wait. She pushed the drawer closed and hurried out the door.

Change In The Air

The room was dark and quiet. Angela was asleep and didn't notice the small alarm clock on the table noiselessly turn to five o'clock. But Izzy saw it. She lay in bed on her back, eyes open, staring into the blackness. It had been a long and restless night, most of it spent in that peculiar state somewhere between wakefulness and sleep. It was hard to tell if the thoughts tumbling around in her head were real or memories or dreams.

Izzy turned on her side and rolled out of bed. Enough of this she thought as she pulled on her robe. She slowly and quietly walked over to the desk along the wall and turned on the small lamp. Angela moaned softly and shifted in the covers. Carefully Izzy opened the top drawer and looked inside but, not finding anything, she slid the drawer closed, opened the bottom drawer, and pulled out a notebook. She pulled back the cover and silently studied the writing inside. Maybe, she thought but she couldn't be sure. She put the the notebook back and rummaged through the rest of the drawer before finally pulling out a small wooden box. She pushed open the metal latch and opened the lid. Inside the box were five small white envelopes and several sheets of matching paper.

"What are you doing?"

The voice startled Izzy and she nearly dropped the box. She looked up and saw Angela laying in bed, propped up on her elbow, staring at her.

"I, um, well," Izzy stammered, "I was looking for some colored pencils. I couldn't sleep and I was going to do my homework. I have to make a map of Europe for Geography class and I need some colored pencils."

Angela threw back the covers and sat up in bed. "They're in the middle drawer," she said.

Izzy put the wooden box back in its' place and clumsily grabbed the pencils out of the drawer. "Thanks Angela," she replied softly, hopeful that Angela really believed her story.

"No problem," she answered. "You can use my stuff anytime you want. After all, I owe you for that awesome hair clip you…."Angela stopped in mid-sentence and gasped. "Izzy!," she cried, "what happened to your hair?"

"I would have thought you would have heard about it," Izzy replied calmly. "I'll give you one guess."

Angela stared at her for a moment until finally her eyes narrowed and her jaw clenched. "Cassandra?"

"Yes, Cassandra," Izzy said. "She put gum in my hair and I had to cut it out."

"Oh Izzy," Angela said as she slid out of bed, leaning against the headboard as she balanced on her good leg. "I went to a play after school with the theater class and you were asleep when I got home. I had no idea. I'm so sorry. I can't believe she would do that! Actually, I can believe she would do that. Cassandra is evil. But your hair still looks good Izzy. It's just shorter."

That's just like Angela Izzy thought. She was so positive and supportive and could always find something good inside of something bad. Angela's thoughtfulness made Izzy feel guilty for having looked into her desk.

"Thanks Angela," Izzy said. "It is what it is I guess. My hair will grow back so I'm not worried about it. Besides, it's Cassandra that needs to be worried, not me."

"Now Izzy," Angela cautioned, "don't do anything crazy. You've already been to Principal Thompkins' office once and spent a week in Room Arrest. You don't need any more trouble."

"Trouble is all I've had since I got here," Izzy replied. "And I don't plan on getting into trouble, I plan on getting out of it." She hadn't been up all night for nothing. Izzy was going to get even with Cassandra Smithton and had come up with a great idea of just how she could do it.

"But Izzy," Angela protested, "you…."

"No Angela," Izzy said sternly, "that's enough. You don't need to worry about it. This isn't your problem and the less you know about it the better. That way you won't get into trouble if anything goes wrong."

Izzy stood up and grabbed her shower bag. "I need to get going," she said. "I want to get to class early so I can talk to Mr. Crandall about an assignment. I'll see you later Angela."

"Okay," Angela answered, "have it your way Izzy. Just be careful."

"Don't worry," Izzy replied as she walked out the door. "I can handle Cassandra Smithton."

Izzy showered quickly and came back to the room just as Angela was leaving to go down to the bathroom to get ready. She changed into her school uniform and then sat down at her desk. She opened the drawer, pulled out the new letter, and copied it into her notebook, hopeful that Mr. Crandall could again help her figure out what it meant. But even if he could tell her what it meant he couldn't tell her who wrote it. She would have to somehow figure that out on her own. Last night she had been fairly certain that it was Tom Andrews. His writing was similar to the writing on the letter and what he had said in his talk about tsunamis was pretty much what the first letter had said. But there were a lot of problems with her theory, like why he would do it and how he could get onto the second floor of the girls dormitory. The doubts had lead Izzy to suspect Angela. Obviously it would be easy for her to leave a letter in the room and her envelopes and stationary were almost identical to those of the letters. But things still didn't make any sense. Why would Angela be writing her strange poems? But if it wasn't Tom or Angela then who was it?

Izzy stuffed the notebook in her backpack and swung the bag onto her shoulder as she headed out the door. She went down to the dining room, grabbed a bagel, and ate it as she walked over to Graham Hall. When she walked into the classroom Mr. Crandall was sitting at his desk grading papers and sipping a cup of coffee.

"Good morning, Mr. Crandall," Izzy said politely.

He looked up from his work and set the coffee cup down on the desk. "Well," he said, "Good morning to you Miss Watson. What brings you to class so early?"

"I've been reading some more poetry and I've come across another poem that I can't quite figure out, Izzy said. "I was hoping you could help me."

"Of course, Isabella," Mr. Crandall replied enthusiastically. "I'd be delighted. Let me have a look."

Mr. Crandall took the notebook from Izzy and carefully studied the poem for several minutes.

"Interesting," he said repeatedly, each time rubbing his chin with his hand. He read the poem aloud to himself and then handed the notebook back to Izzy.

"Tell me, Miss Watson," he said, "what is your interpretation of the poem?"

"I don't know for sure," Izzy replied weakly, "that's why I'm here."

"Come now Isabella," Crandall answered, "you know that I will not simply give you the answer. That would be intellectual laziness. Give me your best guess, such as it is."

Izzy paused for a moment. "Well," she began, "I think it's obvious that the first few lines are saying that there is evil out there, you know, a lot of bad stuff. And the rest of the poem says there are people around that can help you."

"Indeed, Miss Watson, I believe your interpretation is, on the surface at least, correct," Mr. Crandall said. "But there seems to be a bit more to it. For example, who might these people be, the people who can help you?"

"That's the part I don't really get," Izzy answered.

"Well," Mr. Crandall replied slowly, "I would guess that the author is talking about friends and family. The friends are represented by the hands that are put together in friendship and the family by the term "the old one's," which perhaps means parents or grandparents. Thus, the "primal stone" would be the rock-solid foundation of family and friends."

"Yes," Izzy replied as a thought slowly formed in her mind, "That would make sense, wouldn't it?"

"But remember Isabella," Mr Crandall said as he held his finger in the air in front of him, "great poetry often has more than one meaning. There can be other interpretations of this poem that are just as valid and "correct" as the one we have created. And something tells me this poem may indeed have an alternative meaning that you have not yet considered."

Izzy didn't get a chance to ask Mr. Crandall what he thought that "alternative meaning" might be. Their conversation was interrupted by a loud, piercing scream followed quickly by a crashing thud. Izzy and Mr. Crandall ran out into the hallway where several students crowded around another student who lay sprawled on the ground with books and papers scattered around her. Cassandra Smithton!

Cassandra was laying on the floor in front of her locker, crying hysterically. Black mascara ran down her face and, for the first time ever, her hair was messed up. But something else was messed up too. In the middle of her chest was a large lump. At first neither Izzy nor the other students knew what it was but the answer seemed to come to all of them at the same time. Cassandra Smithton stuffed her bra! When she had fallen whatever she had put in her bra shifted position and ended up lumped together in the middle of her chest.

"There's a snake in my locker!," Cassandra screamed. "Somebody put a snake in my locker!"

Cassandra's two ever-present sidekicks helped her to her feet as she wiped her face and struggled to reposition her stuffing. Mr. Crandall walked over to the locker and calmly pulled out a thick brown snake nearly two feet long. Cassandra and the sidekicks howled and backed up against the wall.

"Somebody put that monster in my locker!," Cassandra yelled angrily.

"This is not a monster, Miss Smithton," Mr. Crandall responded. "This is a harmless garden snake. I'm sure that you have scared him nearly as much as he has scared you." He put the snake in a shoe box and handed it to one of the boys to take outside.

"She did it!," Cassandra hissed as she pointed at Izzy. "I know she did. Watson put that thing in my locker!"

"I did not!," Izzy answered defiantly.

"Yes you did, you freak!," Cassandra snarled.

"That is enough, Miss Smithton!," Crandall answered sternly. "I am sure that is not the case. One would guess that it would have been someone that knows the combination to your locker. I would doubt that Miss Watson has that information."

Cassandra continued to protest her case as the crowd slowly drifted away but Mr. Crandall would have none of it. She and her faithful sidekicks finally gave up and stormed off to the bathroom to try to put Cassandra back together again.

The class-bell rang and Izzy and the other students filed into class, laughing quietly and whispering about the spectacle they had just seen. A few minutes later Cassandra walked into the classroom with her make-up re-done, her hair perfect, and her now famous chest back in position. As she settled into the seat behind her Izzy heard the whispered threat – "This isn't over Watson."

Izzy knew her feud with Cassandra Smithton was far from over. She had won a battle but not the war. But Izzy had made up her mind and she was stubborn. Cassandra had pushed her too far and she was going to fight back. She hadn't started all this but she was going to finish it. For now, she was content and just wanted to enjoy her victory.

Izzy waited around after class hoping to get a chance to ask Mr. Crandall what he had meant by an "alternative meaning" to the poem. But several other students went up to his desk to ask about the new assignment so Izzy left and went out into the hall. She walked down to her locker, opened the door, and put away her English notebook. She reached out to grab her geometry book and as she did so she felt a tap on her shoulder.

"Hi Izzy," Tom said.

Izzy turned around and smiled. "Hi Tom."

Tom looked around to make sure no one was watching. "Man Izzy," he said excitedly, "that was awesome! You really hung it on Cassandra. It's about time somebody knocked her down a few pegs and put her in her place."

"I didn't do it," Izzy replied with a smile.

"Oh, okay, I get it," Tom answered. "If that's your story, that's alright. But everybody thinks you're the coolest. They're all talking about how you took down the great Cassandra Smithton."

Izzy kind of liked the sound of that. Everybody thinks I'm cool? That's better than everyone thinking I'm a weirdo. "A girl's gotta do what a girl's gotta do," she said confidently.

"No doubt, Izzy, no doubt," Tom answered. "You know, I was thinking, would you like to go out some-time, maybe watch a movie or something?"

Izzy's face instantly turned red and she stared nervously down at the ground. Tom Andrews is asking me out on a date! She had never been on a date before and, in fact, had never wanted to go on a date before. A few seconds ago she was feeling brash and cocky but now she felt giddy and a bit silly.

"Well, I guess, you know," Izzy stammered, wondering why she had suddenly lost the ability to speak clearly. "We could, you know, if you wanted, we could probably do something like that."

"Does that mean "yes" Izzy?," Tom asked hopefully.

Izzy managed to look up from the floor. "That means yes."

"Cool!," Tom said excitedly. "How 'bout Friday after school?"

"Great," Izzy answered, not wanting to embarrass herself by trying to say anything more.

"Okay, Friday it is," Tom said. "I'll see you later Izzy."

"Okay," she said. "Bye."

Tom turned and walked away down the hall. Izzy let out a deep breath and put her hand to her chest to slow her pounding heart. Suddenly, the bell rang and reminded her that she was still at school. She slammed the locker door and raced off to class.

The rest of the school day was boring and uneventful and Izzy was thankful for that. The drama and excitement of the morning was more than enough and after being up all night she was exhausted. Nobody said anything to her about Cassandra but she knew everyone was talking about it. When she walked down the hall between classes people pointed and watched as she passed by. Before this morning no one had ever seemed to notice her at all, but now they did and some of them even smiled or waved. Now everyone knew Izzy Watson and they knew what she had done. And Izzy enjoyed the attention. It somehow made her feel important. Maybe, she thought, this is what it's like to be popular.

When school got out Izzy went back to her room to start on her homework. She had a lot to do and wanted to get it done so she could go to bed early. She changed out of her uniform and into her pajamas and then climbed onto her bed, leaning back against the headboard. She tried to study but her mind kept bringing up pictures of Tom Andrews. She hadn't really noticed before but he was cute, really cute! And now she had a date with him. What should she wear? How should she act? What if my brain turns to mush again and I mumble like an idiot? What if he tries to kiss me? Izzy's mind raced in circles until finally, reluctantly, she pushed the thoughts aside and started on her homework.

An hour later Angela came in and had Izzy tell her everything that had happened this morning with Cassandra Smithton. Izzy recounted the story in great detail, especially the part about the solitary lump in the middle of Cassandra's blouse. Izzy laughed hysterically until she noticed that Angela wasn't laughing with her.

"What's the matter Angela?," Izzy asked.

"This isn't good, Izzy," Angela replied, "this isn't good at all."

"What?," Izzy cried. "Not good? This is great! She deserved it for what she's done to me and to a lot of other people around here. And everyone agrees with me Angela. They all think it's cool that somebody finally put Cassandra in her place."

Angela looked worried and slowly shook her head. "I don't know Izzy," she said. "I think you've opened Pandora's box."

Izzy stared at her. "What are you talking about?," she asked. "Pandora's box?"

"You know," Angela said, "the Greek mythological story of Pandora. She opened a box and let out all the problems of the world. Once you open the box you can't put the problems back inside either. I think things are just going to get worse Izzy. This hasn't fixed anything."

Izzy was getting a little annoyed. Angela was raining on her victory parade. "Look Angela, don't worry about it," she said calmly. "Cassandra can dish it out but she can't take it. Things will be fine."

Angela didn't respond. She slowly limped over to her bed, sat down, and loosened her leg brace.

"Do you want to hear some good news?," Izzy asked playfully.

"What good news?," Angela replied.

"I have a date," Izzy said proudly.

"A what?," Angela exclaimed. "A date? I thought you didn't like boys?"

"I don't like boys but this particular boy is different," Izzy answered. "He's more mature. He's really nice and he's smart. And he's really cute!"

Angela leaned back in her bed and smiled. "That's great Izzy," she said. "I'm happy for you. Maybe he can protect you from Cassandra."

"Don't be such a worry-wart," Izzy laughed. "I told you, I'll be fine. Don't worry about it."

"I hope so," Angela said as she pushed herself up in bed. "Where are you going on your date?"

"I don't know," Izzy answered. "I guess I'll find out Friday night."

"Friday night?," Angela cried as she sat straight up and stared at Izzy. "You're going out Friday night? We had plans Friday night. Remember? I checked out the DVD player from the library. We were going to have popcorn and watch movies."

"Well, we can do it Saturday night," Izzy said.

"Yeah right," Angela replied. "You know you can never get the DVD player on a Saturday night. Someone always has it reserved on Saturday nights. I almost didn't get it for Friday. Marcia Wilson had it reserved and the only way she would let me have it was if I cleaned her room for her. That's where I've been for the last two hours. And now you say you can't make it?"

"I'm really sorry Angela," Izzy said. "I just forgot, that's all. I'll make it up to you, I promise. We'll do something else."

Angela slid off the bed and grabbed her brace. "That's okay, Izzy," she said as she tightened the brace, "I understand. We all forget things. I'm starving. I'm going to go downstairs and get something to eat. I'll see you later."

Izzy felt bad. She hadn't meant to hurt Angela's feelings. It was a simple mistake and Angela would understand. She always did. Izzy went back to her homework and soon forgot about Angela. But it wasn't as easy to forget about Tom Andrews and after thirty minutes she gave up on her homework.

She'd managed to finish only three geometry problems but had filled half a page with the name "Tom Andrews" surrounded by hearts and stars. She closed her book and dropped it off the edge of the bed. It had been a long day and she was exhausted. She pulled the covers over her head to block the light and went to sleep.

A Thing Called Love

Izzy's hands were trembling. She dropped them to her sides and shook them hard, trying to flick the shakes away as if it was mud on her fingers. But the tremors refused to stop and actually seemed to be spreading. Her heart fluttered along in rhythm with her hands and her breathing picked up the same beat. She felt like she had swallowed an earthquake and it was shaking her apart from the inside out.

Izzy leaned back in the chair, squeezed her eyes shut, and took a deep breath. "This is crazy!," she said out loud to herself. "It's a date, not a firing squad!" She couldn't believe how nervous she was about her date with Tom Andrews and she was frustrated. It wasn't like her to be nervous. Except for her fear of public speaking she never got nervous about anything, ever. In fact, Izzy had always enjoyed her time in the spotlight at big events. It was an opportunity for Izzy to be Izzy, a chance to show other people who and what she was and to feel free to do things her way. And it came from her deeply-held belief that she really, truly, didn't care what other people thought of her. They could like it or hate it, approve or disapprove, take it or leave it. To her it didn't matter one way or the other. Izzy was going to be Izzy.

But now things were different. Now she did care what other people thought of her, especially Tom Andrews. For the first time ever Izzy was concerned with how she looked and what she wore and worried about how to act and what to say. Her previous youthful freedom had been replaced by a teenager's strange but unstoppable desire to look good, act cool, and fit in. And for the last two hours it had been driving her crazy! She had tried on nearly every piece of clothing she had and none of it looked good. Too short, too long, wrong color. For some reason all of her favorite clothes were now incredibly lame and completely awful. And so was her hair. She had spent an hour wrestling with it in an unsuccessful attempt to make it look half-way decent. But the ponytail didn't work and neither did the braids or the curls or the barrets. If anything, her hair looked worse than her clothes.

In her anxiety and frustration Izzy seemed not to notice that it was not her hair or her clothes that had changed. It was her. She had always been different from everyone else, a free-spirit unconcerned with conformity and convention and unafraid to do things her own way. But now her uniqueness, her "Izzy-ness," seemed to be slipping away. Tom Andrews was changing her and her newly-acquired fame from the smackdown of Cassandra Smithton was changing her too. Her boyfriend and her fame meant that she was a somebody now, somebody important. She had become something that until now she had never wanted to be, something that until a few days ago she thought was meaningless and superficial. Izzy was popular. If she needed any proof of all that had changed all she needed to do was look in the mirror. The reflection would have shocked the old Izzy. Staring back was a face decorated with mascara, eye liner, eye shadow, and rouge. Izzy Watson was wearing make-up!

Reluctantly, Izzy put on a yellow shirt with a denim vest and pulled her hair back at the sides, fastening it behind her head with the hair clip she had made for Angela. She still didn't like how she looked but she had to do something. Tom would be coming by to pick her up in five minutes and she wanted to be ready. As she bent down to pull on a pair of black leather boots she was surprised, and somewhat pleased, to notice that her vest was tight across her chest. She stood up and admired her profile in the mirror, happy to see before her the shapely body of a young woman rather than the scrawny outline of a tomboy.

"Hello!"

Izzy jumped and spun around towards the door. "Oh, hi Angela," Izzy answered, embarrassed by Angela's sudden appearance. "I didn't hear you come in."

Angela laughed and grinned at Izzy. "Didn't hear me?," she asked playfully. "You didn't hear me clunking down the hall or hear me open the door? I guess your mind was somewhere else?"

"I guess," Izzy answered sheepishly as she self-consciously stepped away from the mirror.

"Don't worry," Angela said, "you look great. I bet Tom will….." Angela stopped in mid-sentence. She came a few steps closer and stared intently at Izzy. "Are you wearing make-up?," she exclaimed.

"Yea," Izzy said defensively, "so what?"

"No need to get all huffy about it," Angela replied. "It's just, well, it's just kind-of shocking to see you wearing make-up. It's not, you know, it's not your style."

"What would you know about style?," Izzy asked sarcastically. "I have a date and I want to look nice so I put on some make-up. Big deal."

Angela looked at Izzy for a moment but said nothing and slowly limped over to her bed and sat down. Izzy's harsh words hurt but Izzy was too busy rearranging her hair to notice. A few seconds later came a loud knock at the door. Izzy hurried over, took a deep breath, and opened the door.

"Hi Izzy," Tom said.

"Hi Tom," Izzy asnswered nervously.

"Are you ready to go?," he asked.

"Yeah, I'm ready," she replied. "Just let me grab my jacket." Izzy turned and reached for her jacket hanging on the back of the door.

"What's that thing in your hair?," Tom asked loudly.

"What?," Izzy asked as she reached up to cover her hair clip.

"That goofy-looking shiney thing," Tom said with a laugh.

"Oh, this thing?," Izzy answered as she pulled the hair clip out of her hair. "This is Angela's. She thought I should wear it. I didn't want to but she insisted."

Izzy turned around. "Here you go, Angela," she said. "Thanks anyway." Izzy tossed the hair clip high in the air across the room. It bounced on the bed near where Angela was sitting and fell noisily to the floor. "Later."

Tom and Izzy talked and laughed as they left Franklin Hall on their way to Bryson's House on the far north side of the Exeter campus. As freshman they were not allowed to leave campus except with an adult so their choice of where to go on their date was limited. Some students went to the dining room or the library or even to the gymnasium but most people went to Bryson's House, a small stone building that had previously been the home of one of the earliest principals at Exeter Boarding School. It had later been remodeled and turned into a student center where students could go on weekends to relax, hang out with friends and, perhaps most importantly, wear regular clothes instead of school uniforms. It had a fully stocked kitchen where for a small fee students could make their own dinner and down the hall it had a game room, a television room, and a music room, one of the only places on campus where students could listen to their own music. It was run by the senior class and it was their job to make sure that no "immature, immoral, or improper" activities took place. Two senior-class chaparones were always on duty and they took their job very seriously since they were personally responsible for any problems that occurred.

Bryson's House was an oasis, a refuge from the strict and austere campus life at Exeter Boarding School. It was a popular hangout and usually was very busy but for some reason tonight was different. As they walked in Tom and Izzy were surprised to find only three people sitting in the kitchen and the stereo quiet. Neither of them had ever been to Bryson's before but they had heard stories of loud music, dancing, food fights, and headstand contests. They hadn't expected a quiet and nearly empty house.

"Do you want something to drink?," Tom asked.

"Sure," Izzy replied. "I'll take a Dr. Pepper."

Tom went to the machine and got two sodas and then he and Izzy went over to a leather couch along the far wall and sat down. Tom opened his can of soda, the loud "pop" breaking the awkward silence of Bryson's House.

"Man Izzy," Tom exclaimed, "everybody said this place was really cool but it's kind of lame. I'm sorry. We can go somewhere else if you want."

"This is fine," Izzy answered politely. "I don't mind. Besides, it will give us a chance to talk since we never have a chance to talk at school."

They both took a drink from their sodas, each waiting for the other to say something. Izzy searched for something to say but quickly decided that all of her ideas were either silly or stupid.

"She's kind of a weirdo, huh?" Tom finally said.

"Who?," Izzy asked.

"What's her name. Your roommate," he replied.

Izzy wanted to defend Angela but something held her back. "Her name is Angela," Izzy said. "She's okay."

"Maybe so," Tom answered as he leaned back on the couch. "But everyone says she's kinda goofy. And she's got that freaky leg."

Izzy sat quietly. She wanted to stick up for Angela but didn't want Tom to think she was a weirdo too. She wanted Tom to like her and didn't want to argue on their first date. "She's a good roommate," Izzy said meekly.

"If you say so," Tom replied. "But you have to be careful now Izzy. You have to hang out with the right people. After all, you took down the great Cassandra Smithton. The whole school thinks that was great and they think you're really cool."

Izzy was glowing inside. She wasn't "Weirdo Watson" anymore! She was cool. "Well," Izzy said with an air of self-satisfaction, "I hate to admit it but I enjoyed doing it. She deserved it."

"Yea, she did deserve it," he said. "Everybody wishes they could have done what you did but you did it and now you're one of the most popular girls in the freshman class."

"Really?," Izzy said with fake humility. "You really think so?"

"I know so, Izzy," Tom answered. "You're popular now. And in high school that means everything."

Tom leaned forward and took a long drink from the soda can and then looked straight at Izzy. "Don't you get it Izzy? I mean, come on! You've been here long enough to know that status is the only thing that matters to people. No one really cares if you're nice or honest or talented. It's kind of like Brittney Spears or Lindsey Lohan. They aren't nice or honest or even particularly talented but everyone wants to be like them and hang with them because they're popular and famous. It's the same deal in high school. If you're popular you've got it made."

Izzy paused before she said anything, not wanting to say anything wrong. "But," she said slowly, "isn't that kind of a twisted, fake sense of reality? After all, you're saying that it doesn't matter what kind of person you are, that the only thing that counts is what other people think of you."

Tom shrugged his shoulders and took another drink. "I didn't make the rules Izzy," he said, "I just play by'em. And now you have to learn how to play by them too. After all, you're really popular now and you're a Watson."

Izzy was confused. "What's being a Watson got to do with anything?"

Tom laughed. "Girl, you've got a lot to learn!" he said. "Being a Watson means plenty around here. It's like being a Kennedy or something. Watson's are like royalty at Exeter so just being one makes you famous."

"That's just silly," Izzy replied. "It's like I get extra-credit just because of my last name."

"Exactly!," Tom exclaimed loudly. "The Watson name gives you instant status. And you put that together with being beautiful and the smack-down of Cassandra and "Bang!," you're instantly popular."

Izzy liked the part about being beautiful but the rest of it would take a little getting used to. "I'm sure you're right Tom," she said, "but it still seems a little weird."

"Of course it's weird Izzy," Tom laughed, "it's high school."

Tom and Izzy talked for another two hours. They left the subject of high school behind and moved on to other things like music, movies, computers, and sports. The conversation was light and easy and they found they had a lot of things in common. After a while they went to the kitchen to make some popcorn and then sat down to watch a movie. The movie was terrible so they turned it off and tossed popcorn into each others mouths as they sat at opposite ends of the couch. Finally, the senior-class chaperone appeared and told them Bryson's House was closing and they would have to leave. They cleaned up the popcorn misses from the floor and Izzy carefully counted each one so she could prove to Tom that she really had caught more than he did. The chaperone came back and herded them out the front door as if there were a fire in the house.

Tom and Izzy strolled back across campus towards Franklin Hall and sat down on the bench at the bottom of the steps. Everything at Exeter closed down at nine-o'clock and the campus was quiet and still, more so than usual tonight as it was very cold outside. But Tom and Izzy hardly noticed the cold. In fact, they hardly noticed anything around them except for each other. For a few moments their world had shrunk down to only a small park bench and the two of them. Tom leaned in and kissed Izzy on the cheek. A warm flush filled her face and quickly chased away the cold night air. Izzy could have sat on the bench with Tom Andrews forever. But a voice quickly brought her back to reality. Mr. Crandall stood in the doorway of Franklin Hall and politely, but clearly, reminded them of the rules at Exeter Boarding School. Tom immediately stood up, winked at Izzy, and disappeared down the sidewalk and into the darkness.

****

Izzy slept late Saturday morning, not waking up until the room was so bright she couldn't sleep anymore. She slowly rolled over, rubbed her eyes, and looked at the clock. Ten-thirty. She had promised Angela that she would get up at eight-o'clock and go to the girls volleyball game with her to make-up for ruining their plans last night. Angela had tried to wake her up but Izzy had pushed her away. She was tired and didn't want to go to a stupid volleyball game. Nobody went to the volleyball games, at least nobody that was cool. Besides, she was annoyed with Angela. She had tried to tell her all about her date when she got in last night but Angela hadn't seemed very interested, at least not as interested as Izzy thought she should be.

Izzy reluctantly rolled out of bed and stretched her arms high above her head. It was bright and sunny outside, the first nice day in nearly a week. She shuffled slowly over to her desk and sat down to brush her hair, her mind filled with thoughts of last night and her first date. Tom was cute, really cute, and nice and smart and funny. Her sides still hurt from laughing so hard. Izzy stopped brushing her hair and stared at herself in the mirror. Beautiful, huh? She had never thought of herself as beautiful before nor had she ever thought of herself as ugly. Until the last few days she hadn't particularly thought of herself at all.

What was that thing Link used to say- "Beauty is only skin deep. What matters is on the inside, not the outside." Well, apparently Link was wrong. Tom Andrews had said just the opposite. High school was all about the outside. Nobody cared about the inside.

Izzy put down the hair brush and walked over to her armoire. She slid open the bottom drawer and brought out two shoe boxes and then went over to the door where she began taking down the decorations she had put up to add color and character to the room. She pulled down the beads and placed them in the box and threw the dried flowers in the trash. The decorations strung across the back of the headboards fell to the ground as she cut the string holding them in place. She picked up the colored socks and put them in a box and took all of her hair bands and necklaces and stuffed them in the box with the beads. She quickly shuffled through the pictures that had hung from the headboard – a dog, a bear, a jungle, an orange sunset. How silly and childish she thought as she wadded them up and stuffed them in the trash. The door opened just as Izzy put the lids on the shoe boxes.

"What are you doing, Izzy?," Angela cried as she walked into the room.

"I'm taking all this stuff down," Izzy answered.

"But why?," Angela asked. "It makes the room bright and colorful. It makes it come alive!"

"It makes it look childish and immature," Izzy replied sharply.

"No it doesn't," Angela protested. "The beads, the colors, your handmade jewelry. It's unique and it's pretty."

"No Angela, it's lame," Izzy said. "Anyway, it's my room and I can do what I want." She walked across the room to where Angela was standing and shoved one of the boxes at her. "Here," she said. "You can have this stuff. I don't want it anymore."

Angela took the box and lifted off the lid. "Oh, Izzy," she said softly. "This is all of your favorite jewelry. You made these things yourself. I can't take this."

"Take it Angela," Izzy ordered, "all of it. I don't want it anymore."

Angela closed the box and carried it over to her bed. Izzy went to her armoire, took off her pajamas, and changed into a pair of jeans and a yellow sweater. Neither girl said a word. Izzy finished dressing, grabbed her backpack and her coat, and walked over to the door. "I'm going to the library to work on some homework," she said as she opened the door. "Just consider that stuff a payback for me screwing up your plans last night and your having to clean Marcia Wilson's room. We're even now."

Izzy closed the door, hurried downstairs, and walked out of Franklin Hall into the bright sunshine. Tom had mentioned that he might be going to the library this morning and she hoped she hadn't missed him. The sun was already beginning to warm the air and the afternoon would be perfect for a walk, assuming of course that she could "accidentally" run into Tom at the library. She marched quickly along the sidewalk, head down, oblivious to everything around her. She needed to think of something to say to Tom if she did find him so she wouldn't look too obvious. She didn't know much about dating but she did know it wasn't "cool" to seem too eager.

"Hello Isabella."

Izzy stopped abruptly and looked up. “Oh, hi Iam,” she said casually. “I didn’t see you there.”

“How can you see anything when you walk along staring at your shoes?,” Iam said with a laugh. “You should be looking around at the sky and the trees on such a beautiful day.”

“Yea, I guess I should,” Izzy replied indifferently, annoyed that she had run into Iam and anxious to be on her way.

Iam laid down his shovel and sat down on a large pile of dirt. “How have you been Isabella?,” he asked.

“I’ve been okay,” she replied quickly.

“Yes, that’s what I’ve heard,” he said “I can’t go anywhere around here without hearing your name.”

Izzy relaxed a little and smiled. “Everyone’s talking about me, huh?,” she said, her voice showing more than a hint of pride. “At least now they’re saying good things instead of calling me “Weirdo Watson.”

“Yes, they are saying a lot of good and flattering things about you lately,” Iam said, “but aren’t these the same people who were saying a lot of bad things about you just last week? What’s changed?”

“A lot of things have changed,” Izzy answered. “And for the better too. I’ve got it figured out now. I know what I need to do, what I need to be.”

Iam furrowed his brow and looked at Izzy. “You know what you need to be?,” he asked. “Shouldn’t you just be yourself?”

“Don’t be so naïve, Iam,” Izzy snapped. “I already tried that and it didn’t work.”

“And you think this will?,” Iam asked calmly.

Izzy's eyes narrowed and a look of scorn and contempt spread across her face. She'd heard enough. Iam was nice and she liked him but she wasn't going to listen to a lecture. It was as if Iam was her parents, Link, and Angela all rolled into one and it was getting on her nerves. She didn't need this, not now.

"Look Iam," Izzy said loudly, "I know what I'm doing. I took care of Cassandra Smithton, didn't I? If I would have listened to you and Angela I'd still be "Weirdo Watson."

Iam stood up slowly and picked up his shovel. "Everything has a price Isabella, including fame," he said. "Be careful of what you might lose along the way."

Izzy had heard enough. Lose along the way? She hadn't lost a thing! She had gained. Friends. A boyfriend. Popularity. She was winning, not losing.

"I'll see you later," Izzy said as she turned to walk away.

"Maybe you could stop by and see us sometime," Iam called as she walked off. "Gabriel misses you."

"If I can find the time," Izzy called over her shoulder. "I'll let you know."

Izzy marched quickly towards the library, angered by Iam's lecture and irritated by the wasted time. It was nearly eleven-forty-five and Tom might already be gone. She jogged up the steps and into the library and went over to a desk along the far wall. She set down her backpack, peeled off her jacket, and pulled out one of her notebooks. If she did run into Tom she at least needed to look like she was at the library to study.

She self-consciously straightened her hair and her shirt as she slowly looked around the library but not seeing anything she got up and began walking the aisles. She started at the bookcase marked "A" and casually strolled down each aisle, slowly looking to the left and then to the right, and stopping occasionally as she pretended to look for a book. By the time she reached the "XYZ" aisle Izzy was frustrated. There was no sign of Tom Andrews. In her frustration and near desperation she was able to convince herself that he must be in the boys bathroom. But after standing as inconspicuously as possible next to the door for ten minutes with no results, she finally gave up. She went back to the desk feeling disappointed and more than a little foolish. Izzy tossed her notebook onto the desk and slumped down in the chair. This is crazy, hanging around by the bathroom like that she thought. What's wrong with me? She tossed her head backward and let out a deep breath. When she brought her head back down, however, her breathing completely stopped and her hands clutched the edge of the desk.

Laying on the desktop next to her backpack was a small white envelope with neat black writing that read "Miss Isabella Watson." Izzy quickly looked around to find who had left it, hoping of course to see Tom Andrews walking away. But she didn't see anyone. Her fingers shook as she opened the envelope and unfolded the letter.

All The World Is Indeed A Stage
It Has Not Changed From Age To Age
The Actress Comes To Play Her Part
Yet Often Leaves A Broken Heart
She Lives Inside What Is Not Real
And Loves The Things That Cannot Heal
The Heart Belongs To The One Above
He Is The One Who Deserves Your Love
You Must Act In A Different Play
One That Lasts Beyond This Day
It Has All That You Desire
Play The Part And Escape The Fire

Izzy read the letter a second time, and then a third, and then calmly layed it on the desk. This one, unlike the first two, made sense. She wasn't completely sure of the meaning of each line but she was certain about the meaning of the poem. It was obviously a love note from Tom Andrews! It had to be! The actress in the play was a girl in high school. What was high school if not one big drama? And the line "The Heart Belongs To The One Above"? That meant her heart belonged to Tom since he was nearly a year older than her and taller. And he was telling her to play the part that was assigned to her, the part of a Watson at Exeter Boarding School. If she did, she would have everything she desired and "escape the fire," the hell, of being "Weirdo Watson."

Suddenly, Izzy remembered that she had copies of the first two poems in her backpack. They were still there from when she had taken them to Mr. Crandall. She quickly pulled them out and read the first poem.

See Not The Air That Gives You Breath
Yet Without It Certain Death
You Pass It By But Do Not See
Does That Mean It Cannot Be?
The Desert Boy He Sees Not Snow
Does That Mean No Blizzards Blow?
How Many Things The Hand Can't Feel
This Does Not Mean They Are Not Real
You Cannot See If You Close Your Eyes
Open Them If You Wish Be Wise

Izzy's eyes were open now and she could clearly see the meaning of the poem. Tom was in her English class and geometry class but at first she hadn't noticed him. But he had been watching her the whole time and had obviously written her the poem to tell her to look around and notice him. She grabbed the copy of the second poem and read it.

The Age-Old Battle Rages On
The Evil One Is Never Gone
A Roaring Lion Is On The Prowl
Do Not Run When You Hear His Growl
Stand Tall Upon The Primal Stone
Remember That You Are Not Alone
Use The Strength That Last Forever
The Hands Have Power When Put Together
The Old Ones Speak An Ancient Tongue
Use Their Words To Fight This One

This poem was a little tougher but after a while the meaning became clear too. The "Battle" is the timeless struggle between men and women. The "evil one" and the "roaring lion"must mean that another boy liked her and Tom was telling her not to go out with him. Izzy had no idea what "primal stone" meant but that didn't bother her. It was obvious that the last four lines were talking about love, after all wasn't the line "The Old One's Speak An Ancient Tongue" a clear reference to the "language of love"? And the line about the hands obviously meant a loving touch or joining hands in marriage.

Izzy could hardly believe it! How could she have been so blind? It was clear now that Tom was crazy about her and had written the letters. She almost felt bad that it had taken her so long to figure it out. She'd probably hurt his feelings by never mentioning the poems and he might be wondering if she really liked him or not. Now that she knew she couldn't wait to thank him and tell him how wonderful his poems were.

Izzy folded the papers and carefully slid them back into her notebook. As she put the notebook into her backpack she suddenly had an idea. Yes, she thought, he would love it! Izzy pulled out a sheet of paper and began writing.

Switching Sides

The stone walls of Franklin Hall were nearly two feet thick but even that wasn't enough to block the sound of the wind as it howled outside. A Nor'easter had blown in on Sunday and as Izzy got ready for school on Tuesday morning it still showed no signs of letting up. The temperature hadn't been able to climb past ten degrees and the snow piled up on the north side of the building nearly to the bottom of the window. The wind pushed the snow horizontally through the air and made it impossible to see more than a few feet. The weather was so bad that classes had been cancelled on Monday, the first snow-day at Exeter Boarding School in twenty-two years.

Izzy didn't pay any attention to the weather outside. She'd been through plenty of blizzards before and would make it through this one. Besides, it was plenty warm in the girls bathroom as she sat in front of the mirror putting on her make-up. Several girls were still in the shower and hot, steamy air rolled over the tops of the shower doors warming the entire room. Izzy was a little annoyed that the humidity was making her hair fuzzy and unmanageable but she welcomed the warmth. She was nearly done with her eye-shadow when she felt someone tap her on the shoulder.

Izzy turned around to see Cassandra Smithton standing behind her with two of her side-kicks alongside. "Hello Cassandra," Izzy said warily.

"Hi Izzy," Cassandra replied. Izzy thought she must have gotten mascara in her eye because it looked like Cassandra was smiling at her! "I'm sorry to bother you Izzy but I'd like to talk to you about something," Cassandra said, still smiling broadly.

"Okay," Izzy answered slowly, "What is it?"

"Well," Cassandra said, "you know I am the captain of the cheerleading team. Last week we had to remove one of the girls from the team for, well, for several different reasons. The girls and I have talked and we would love for you to be on the team. We are having a special tryout today after school and if you come I'm sure I could, you know, arrange things for you."

Now Izzy was really confused. First Cassandra had smiled at her and now this! Maybe she had gotten water in her ears when she took a shower and wasn't hearing correctly. "You want me to be a cheerleader?" she asked skeptically.

"Yes," Cassandra said proudly, "we would be honored to have you on the team. As I said, we all talked about it and it was unanimous."

Izzy stared at Cassandra. "Unanimous means everybody," she said. "Does that mean you too?"

"It does indeed," Cassandra said politely. "Please Izzy, let's put the past in the past. The girls and I were only testing you to see if you had what it takes to be a cheerleader. We only want the best of the best on the team. Please accept my personal apology and my personal invitation to join the team. Our team needs people of your caliber and status."

For a moment Izzy was suspicious and unsure but then she remembered what Tom had said about high school. Status is everything. Izzy had status now, and a famous name, and Cassandra Smithton and the cheerleading team needed her. She reached out and shook Cassandra's hand. "I accept your apology and your invitation," Izzy said proudly. "Thank you very much."

"No, thank you Izzy," Cassandra replied. "See you after school in the gym." She turned and walked out of the bathroom, her two servants following along behind.

Izzy hurriedly finished putting on her make-up and fixed her hair. She needed to get back to her room to pack some gym clothes in her bag for the tryout. She had no idea what she would have to do but that didn't really seem to matter. From the sound of it it seemed clear that Cassandra would take care of everything. She couldn't wait to tell Tom the good news and to thank him for everything. After all, he had explained the rules of high school success to her and she was quickly learning how to use them to her advantage.

Izzy went back to her room to get ready for class. She pulled on her school uniform and stepped into her shoes, ignoring the winter boots sitting beside them. Despite the snow and the cold there was no way she was going to wear them. They were clumsy and ugly and definitely not cool. She stuffed a pair of sneakers and a tee-shirt into her backpack but her shorts were wrinkled. She obviously couldn't wear wrinkled shorts to the cheerleading tryouts so she walked over to Angela's armoire. Izzy opened the top drawer and pulled out a pair of blue shorts.

"What are you doing?"

Izzy looked over her shoulder and saw Angela standing in the doorway. "You said I could borrow your stuff anytime I wanted to," Izzy said.

"You can," Angela replied as she limped over to her desk and sat down. "I'm just wondering what you want with a pair of shorts when there's three feet of snow on the ground and it's ten degrees outside."

Izzy closed the drawer, walked over to her desk, and shoved the shorts into her bag. "I have cheerleading tryouts today after school and I need a pair of shorts," she said. "Mine are dirty."

"You have what?," Angela cried.

"Are you deaf or something?," Izzy sneered. "Cheerleading tryouts! You know, "rah-rah!"?"

"I heard what you said," Angela replied, ignoring Izzy's rudeness. "I just can't believe you said it. You've never wanted to be a cheerleader. What happened?"

"Cassandra asked me to join the team," Izzy answered smugly.

Angela looked down at the floor and shook her head. "You let Cassandra Smithton talk you into trying out for cheerleading?," she asked in disbelief. "You're crazy! What, are you two friends now or something?"

"As a matter of fact we are," Izzy replied, annoyed by the tone of Angela's voice. "She apologized to me and I accepted her apology. You should applaud me for being such a forgiving person. And besides, Cassandra is very nice once you get to know her."

"Nice like a cat is nice and plays with the mouse before he kills it," Angela said.

"Knock it off Angela! I thought you were my friend," Izzy said cynically. "Your just jealous."

Angela laughed. "Jealous?," she said. "I don't think so. I'm just worried about you Izzy. I know Cassandra is up to something. I just don't know what it is."

"No she's not," Izzy protested. "I told you. We're friends now and they need me on their team. And you don't need to worry. If anything happens, which it won't, I can handle Cassandra. I've done it before."

Izzy had heard enough. Listening to Angela was worse than listening to one of Iam's lectures. The two of them were driving her crazy! Always picking at her, annoying her, telling her what she should do or what she shouldn't do. She didn't need a nanny. She was mature, knew what she was doing, and could take care of herself. Who were they to tell her what to do? They didn't know anything about high school and didn't even understand. If she was going to listen to anyone it would be Tom Andrews. He knew how things worked. And so did Cassandra Smithton.

Izzy put on her coat, grabbed her backpack, and walked out the door without saying another word to Angela. As soon as she stepped outside of Franklin Hall the wind hit her like a freight-train and she pulled her head down between her shoulders as she plunged through the snow. It wasn't a long walk over to Graham Hall but by the time she got there Izzy was half-frozen and barely had time to get to the bathroom to fix her hair before the bell rang. She smiled at Cassandra as she took her seat and tried to make eye contact with Tom but he was looking the other way. Izzy's mind wasn't on English this morning and she nearly fell asleep until the sound of the bell brought her out of her drowsiness. Izzy packed-up her notebook and went out into the hall, arriving at her locker at the same time Tom did.

"Hi Izzy," Tom said.

"Hello Tom," Izzy replied as she unpacked her backpack. "How's it goin?"

"Good," he answered. "I heard the news Izzy. Congratulations!"

"Thanks Tom," Izzy said cheerfully. "Isn't it awesome!"

"It's way cool, Izzy, way cool," Tom answered. "You're going to be a cheerleader. And I'm going to be dating a cheerleader. That's cool too."

Izzy leaned against her locker and looked at Tom. "It's time for your actress to play her part," she said with a coy smile.

Tom stared at her. "What?"

"You know," she answered teasingly. "I can see now and I'm ready for the age-old battle."

Tom continued to stare blankly. "Are you okay?," he asked.

"I couldn't be better," Izzy said. "Why?"

"Because you're acting a little weird," he said.

"Oh come on," Izzy said playfully. "You know what I mean."

"Izzy, really," Tom sputtered, "I don't......"

"Mr. Andrews!"

Tom and Izzy quickly looked in the direction of the voice and saw Mr. Crandall standing in the doorway of the English room. "Yes, sir, Mr. Crandall," Tom replied.

"Could I talk with you for a moment please, Mr. Andrews?" Mr. Crandall asked.

Tom smiled at Izzy and shrugged his shoulders. "Yes sir," he answered and walked away.

Izzy waved goodbye and turned back to her locker. I must have caught him off-guard she thought to herself. He obviously wasn't expecting to hear quotes from his poems, especially with other people around. He's probably shy about it and afraid that people will make fun of him. After all, great poets are known to be a little sensitive and tender. Izzy smiled at the thought, closed her locker, and headed for her next class.

The rest of the school day was boring and uneventful. Izzy was disinterested and only wanted to get the day over with and get over to the gym for the tryouts. Her last class seemed to drag on forever and Izzy felt like she was going to explode. Slowly, painfully slowly, the hands on the clock turned until they reached three-thirty and the bell rang, releasing her from her prison.

Izzy immediately got up from her desk and hurried out of the room and down the hall to her locker. She put on her coat and rushed outside into the wind and snow without bothering to zip it. Fortunately, the gym was directly across the courtyard from Graham Hall and Izzy covered the distance quickly.

A few minutes later she emerged from the dressing room and walked out onto the basketball court. She sat down cross-legged on the floor and began to stretch her legs. She wasn't sure what happened at a cheerleading tryout but she figured she would have to jump and kick and she wanted to be ready. As she stretched other girls came out onto the court and began to warm-up. Izzy smiled and wished them good-luck but otherwise kept to herself as she stretched and tried to keep herself from getting nervous. There were a lot more girls trying out then she thought there would be and some of them were really good. She watched them warm up as she stretched and they were doing moves she'd never seen before!

"Attention, attention everyone," Cassandra yelled. She and four other cheerleaders stood near a table on the far side of the court. "Thank you for coming out to the cheerleading trials. We have a great turnout today. There are a total of twenty-seven candidates but as you know there is only one open spot on the team so the competition will be intense. Are you girls ready?"

Everyone around her threw their arms in the air or kicked their legs as they yelled "Yea!" but Izzy didn't move.

"Good, very good," Cassandra said. "Here's how it works. Everyone gets a minute to do their routine. There are three required moves- a herkie, a toe-touch, and a tumbling move. You can add other things but you have to do those three. And of course we need to hear you cheer. It needs to be loud and it needs to be strong. We want to hear some spirit!"

Again everyone jumped and kicked as they yelled but Izzy stood looking straight ahead.

"Alright!," Cassandra yelled. "We'll go in alphabetical order. Lisa Armstrong, you're up!"

Izzy felt nauseated. She didn't know what a herkie was and she certainly didn't know any cheers. She could do a cartwheel and a back handspring but what was she supposed to do about the rest of it? Izzy slowly managed to calm herself down. She could do this. All she had to do was watch the other girls and see what they were doing. It didn't matter whether she knew the names of the moves or not as long as she could do them. She watched a few of the girls do their routines and studied their jumps, watching where they put their arms and how they kicked their legs. She went to the end of the gym and practiced the moves until she thought she had them down. It was almost her turn to go so Izzy walked back down the floor and watched two more routines, amazed by how good they were.

"Our last competitor is Izzy Watson," Cassandra called out. "Come on Izzy, show us what you've got!"

Izzy ran to the middle of the floor and began to work her arms like she had seen the other girls do. She did four front-kicks and then began her cheer as she continued to flail her arms.

"Come on in, give it a try
But you'll lose, I'll tell you why
We got strength, We got speed
We got power, All we need
You can't win, Ain't no doubt
Exeter's gonna knock you out!"

Izzy jumped into the air with her left arm stretched up in the air and her right leg bent up behind her. She landed and immediately jumped back into the air, stretching her arms out to the side, and doing the splits with her legs. When she landed she turned and raced down the center of the floor, stopped, and did a front-flip. On her way back up the floor she did three back-handsprings and finally landed in the center of the floor in the splits with her arms held high in the air.

Izzy stood up. She heard a few people clapping politely but she didn't hear the loud cheering that some of the other girls received when they finished their routines. She slowly walked back to where the other girls were standing and waited while Cassandra and the other judges huddled around the table.

"Okay everybody!," Cassandra finally yelled. "Great job. All of you were wonderful but as I said before we only have one spot. It was a tough competition but we've made our decision. The newest member of the Exeter Freshman Cheerleading Team is.....Izzy Watson!"

Polite applause filled the gym as Izzy made her way over to the table. A few of the other girls congratulated her but most of them simply turned and walked away. Cassandra gave Izzy a hug and tied a large red ribbon in her hair.

"Great job Izzy," Cassandra said. "I knew you could do it."

"Thanks Cassandra," Izzy said. "Thanks to all of you for choosing me. This is a real honor."

"Izzy, Izzy!"

Izzy turned around and saw Tom running across the floor. As he came up to her he wrapped his arms around her and picked her up as he spun around in a circle. "Way to go Izzy!'" he cried as he set her down. "You were great!"

"Thanks," Izzy replied, beaming. "I didn't know how well I did. There wasn't much cheering so I figured I bombed."

"Ah," Tom said, "don't worry about those other girls. They're just jealous. You were clearly the best."

"Well thank you. That's sweet of you to say," Izzy answered. "And thanks for coming here to support me. That's sweet too."

"No problem," Tom replied, "I wouldn't have missed it for the world. I mean, how cool is this. My girlfriend is a cheerleader!"

Izzy's heart skipped a beat when she heard the word "girlfriend" and she flashed Tom a flirtatious smile.

"But I had another reason for coming over here," Tom said. He grabbed Izzy by the arm and led her away from Cassandra and the other girls. "The Christmas Dance is Saturday night and I was hoping we could go together."

Izzy fought hard to control her excitement. She nearly giggled but managed to stop herself. "No thanks," she said.

Tom's eyes got huge and his mouth gaped open. "But, but I thought....."

Izzy laughed and grabbed his arm. "I'm just teasing you, silly," Izzy said. "Of course I'll go with you. I am your girlfriend, aren't I?"

The color came back to Tom's face and he playfully punched Izzy in the arm. "That wasn't funny, Izzy," he said. "I almost swallowed my gum."

"Sorry," Izzy replied with a laugh, "I couldn't resist."

"I'll pick you up in the atrium of Franklin Hall about seven o'clock," Tom said.

"That would be great," Izzy said. She looked around to make sure no one was watching and then grabbed Tom by the arm, pulled him close, and kissed him on the cheek. "I'll see you then."

"Uh, yea, okay Izzy," Tom stammered, looking shocked and a bit embarrassed. "I'll see you then."

Tom walked backward as few steps, still staring at Izzy, and then stopped. He jumped up and punched the air with his fist as he yelled "Yea!" and then he turned and ran out of the gym.

A Dance To Remember

It was cold outside, only twenty-eight degrees, but fortunately the wind was down to just a soft southwesterly breeze. The sun hung low in a cloudless sky, too low to offer much warmth but so bright as it reflected off the snow that it made Izzy squint as she ran. She ran along slowly, breathing heavily and cursing herself for being so out of shape. Before she had come to Exeter she could run or bike or swim all day without getting tired. Now, after only ten minutes of running, she was panting and sputtering and could feel the sharp twinge of a cramp under her right rib cage.

Izzy stopped at the corner of the fence near the gate to Iam's house and bent over, her hands on her knees as she gasped for air. Despite the cold weather she was boiling hot and felt the chill of the sweat as it ran down the middle of her back. She pushed back the hood of her jacket and pulled the sweaty gloves off her hands, dropping them onto the snow. After a few minutes of panting and wheezing her breathing slowed and she felt a little better, though she was still lightheaded and dizzy.

But that was no big deal. Izzy had felt lightheaded and dizzy for almost three days now, ever since she had quit eating.

It had been a lot worse the first day but by now she was almost used to it. The dizziness and the twisting pangs in her stomach were just proof that her crash diet was working and she was losing weight. She had to look good at the dance tonight so she could impress Tom and Cassandra and a little dizziness and some stomach pains weren't going to stop her.

Izzy peeled off her jacket and dropped it on the snow next to her gloves, hopeful that without all of the extra clothes she could run more easily. She opened the latch, stepped quickly through the gate, and closed it behind her. She needed to keep running so she could sweat off a few more pounds but didn't want to run on campus where someone might see her. Her hair was a mess, her nose was running, and she wasn't wearing any make-up. No one needed to see her like this. It wasn't cool.

Izzy took a deep breath and started down the trail. It was covered with snow but she knew the trail well enough that she could easily follow it as it wound through the trees. When she reached the river she turned and followed it upstream until the trail again turned back uphill into the trees. As she trudged slowly up the hill she heard a noise, a faint sound that was difficult to hear over the loudness of her breathing. She heard it again and then again as it moved closer until finally she was sure that she was hearing something. Izzy stopped and listened but by now she didn't need to hear it in order to know what it was. She could see it, a yellow dog running through the snow and barking loudly as he raced through the trees. Gabriel came up beside Izzy and sat down, his wagging tail creating a snow angel behind him.

"Oh, it's just you Gabriel," Izzy said. "For a moment there I was getting a little scared." Izzy turned and began to jog up the hill. "You go home Gabriel," she called over her shoulder. "I'm busy and I don't have time to play with you. Go on!"

Izzy continued up the hill but soon noticed that Gabriel was running along beside her. "Go home!," Izzy yelled as she ran. "Get!" She ran faster and finally reached the top of the hill only to find Gabriel sitting on the trail in front of her holding a stick in his mouth.

"No way Gabriel," Izzy said as she huffed and puffed. "I'm not going to play fetch with you. I'm busy. Now go away!"

"Careful Isabella, you'll hurt his feelings."

Izzy jumped and spun around towards the voice. Iam sat on a rock about fifty feet away near a large stack of firewood, his chainsaw and a lunch pail sitting in the snow beside him. Gabriel walked over to the woodpile and dropped the stick.

"I don't mean to hurt his feelings," Izzy replied. "But he's annoying me. I'm really busy! I have a lot to do today."

Iam patted Gabriel on the head and looked calmly at Izzy. "Indeed, you are very busy these days Isabella. Cheerleading, a boyfriend, your schoolwork. That's a lot. But are you really too busy to eat?"

Izzy groaned. "You're as bad as Angela," she said. "She's been bugging me about it for three days and it's getting on my nerves. You guys just don't understand."

Iam smiled. "Try me," he said.

"Fine!" Izzy said angrily, "if you really want to know, here's the deal. I need to look good at the dance and right now, I don't. I need to lose some weight. I'm fat."

"Fat?," Iam exclaimed in obvious disbelief. "You, fat? I hardly think so Isabella. You've always been thin. At your age your body may be developing and changing but you certainly haven't gotten fat. No one in their right mind would ever say that you are fat."

"Well, I say I am and that's all that matters," Izzy said sharply.

"Just because you say you're fat doesn't make it true," Iam replied. "You can say you're a purple monkey but that doesn't make you one. Anyone can see that you are not a purple monkey. And you're not fat."

"Whatever!," Izzy said with more than a touch of irritation. "That's just how I see it."

Iam paused and let out a long sigh. "Isabella, a person can get very confused trying to figure out who they are, especially at your age," he said. "Some try to figure it out by comparing themselves to others, especially to people who are rich or famous or talented or popular. When they compare themselves to others they usually come up short and feel like they aren't as pretty or as smart or as rich or as skinny. And that can rob you of the joy of just being you, of being that special and wonderful person that only you can be. Instead, you try to become like them and you lose your specialness, your uniqueness, your "Izzy-ness."

"I haven't lost anything," Izzy answered angrily. She was tired of listening to another of Iam's useless lectures and had heard enough. "The only thing I've lost is the name "Weirdo Watson." If you don't like it, or Angela doesn't like it, well that's just too bad! I like it and that's all that really matters. You and Angela need to just leave me alone!"

Izzy turned and ran back down the hill.

****

Mirrors don't lie but in this particular instance Izzy wished that they did. Her hair looked awful and despite an hour of curling, braiding, brushing, and blow drying, it still looked awful. She couldn't understand it. She never had trouble making her hair look good. Her hair had always been one of her best qualities and since the third grade people had always complimented her about it. But tonight Izzy hated it. Too flat, too curly, too straight, too long, too short. It was driving her crazy!

Her make-up had apparently teamed-up with her hair in some kind of mischievious battle against her and was behaving as badly as her hair. Somehow the eye-shadow on her right eye was a slightly different shade than that on her left eye and she'd had to re-do it three times before it finally matched. She struggled with the rouge on her cheeks, alternating between the bright red glow of a clown and the pale white look of a cadaver. The lipstick seemed to be the only non-combatant, at least until Izzy remembered that she hadn't brushed her teeth and had to re-do it.

But her hair and her make-up weren't the worst problem. It was her clothes. Who knew there were so many different shades of red? Her dress was red but certainly not the same color red as her shoes or her lipstick. After a few frantic moments Izzy was able to solve the shoe problem by switching to a black dress. But she soon found out that she obviously couldn't wear "that" necklace with a black dress, setting off a frenzied search that finally ended in Angela's jewelry box. The eye shadow and lipstick were changed one last time and the appropriate bracelet, watch, and rings were obtained, again by a visit to Angela's jewelry box. Finally, Izzy stepped back and admired herself in the mirror. Not bad she thought to herself, not bad at all.

Izzy walked over to her armoire to get her coat and heard Angela open the door and walk into the room. Angela went over to her bed and sat down but Izzy didn't say a word.

"You look nice," Angela said softly.

"Oh," Izzy replied indifferently, "thank you."

"Please be careful with that necklace," Angela said. "My mother gave that to me."

"Don't worry about it," Izzy said casually, "it'll be fine." Izzy closed the doors of the armoire and turned around.

Angela nearly gasped but quickly covered her mouth with her hand. She knew it wouldn't do any good but she felt like she had to say something. "Izzy," she said calmly, "don't you think you should button the front of your dress up a little more?"

Izzy looked down at herself and then glared at Angela. "Come on Angela!," Izzy cried, "you gotta grow up! Don't be so old-fashioned. This is the style nowadays. I think it looks great. You've got to learn to be more open-minded."

Angela grabbed a book and leaned back in her bed. "My grandpa once said that an open mind just meant that all your good ideas could fall out and a bunch of dumb ideas could get in. Better to have a closed mind with a door. New ideas can still come in but only if they have a key to the door. He said the key was common sense and morality."

Izzy rolled her eyes. "Whatever Angela," she huffed. "I'm outta here. Later!"

Izzy left the room, walked down the hall, and stopped at the top of the staircase. She looked over the railing down into the atrium and could see a line of boys along the wall, dressed nicely in suits and looking uncomfortable as they waited for their dates. Izzy could see Tom in the center of the line, fidgeting with his tie as he held a white box with his other hand. Izzy walked slowly down the stairs, her eyes fixed on Tom, hoping he would see her as she descended the steps. But Tom was busy talking and didn't see Izzy until she was nearly at his side. When he saw her he smiled and straightened his tie.

"Hi Izzy," he said nervously, "you look great!"

"Thank you Tom," Izzy replied politely. "You look quite handsome yourself."

"Here," Tom said as he thrust the white box at Izzy. "I got this for you."

Izzy thanked him as she took the box and opened it. Inside was a corsage, a yellow carnation surrounded by white asters and small, green leaves. She laughed flirtatiously as Tom clumsily attempted to pin the flower on her dress and, when he couldn't do it, she pinned it on herself as Tom stood by, nervous and red-faced. She smiled at his shyness but Izzy knew how he felt. She had never experienced the sharp nervousness of romance before but she could feel it now. She felt the lump in her throat, the sweat in her palms, and could sense the excited giggle that tried to come out each time she looked at Tom. Hurriedly, they put on their coats and left Franklin Hall, each trying to escape the awkwardness and discomfort of the moment.

The dance was being held in the school gymnasium but as Izzy and Tom walked in it was hard to tell that this was an old gymnasium. The Student Council had gone all out in decorating it to look like a beach scene. The walls were covered with tall curtains and cardboard cutouts and each wall was different. The far wall was a turquoise-blue ocean topped by a sunset sky while the left wall was a white sand beach with palm trees and the opposite wall was covered with sailboats. The near wall looked like a jungle, complete with hanging stuffed animals including monkeys, parrots, and toucans and along the wall was a row of tables covered with punch bowls and food. The basketball goals at each end of the gym were even decorated, one to look like the moon and the other covered with stars. The lights were turned down and some kind of funky reggae music filled the gym. A few adventurous souls were out on the dance floor but most of the students huddled near the tables.

Tom asked if Izzy wanted to dance but she politely declined. She loved to dance but had no idea how to dance to reggae music, especially in a dress. Instead, they went over to the tables and joined a group of Tom's friends. Izzy didn't know any of them and stood quietly as Tom and his friends talked and laughed about some event that she knew nothing about. The conversation dragged on and Tom failed to notice that Izzy was feeling not only awkward but bored. She tapped him on the arm several times but he was too involved in the conversation to notice. Izzy stood for a while longer, looking around at the decorations, but finally gave up and went to get a glass of punch.

As Izzy stood in line at the punch bowl she noticed the other tables lined up along the wall. They were covered with food! She quickly turned away as she tried to ignore them but her stomach had other ideas. She hadn't eaten in nearly four days and the sight of all that food so close was just too much.

Izzy turned and looked back over her shoulder. Tom was still locked in an animated discussion with his friends and had yet to notice that she was gone. She stepped out of the line for the punch bowl and walked slowly over to the next table. It was covered with all kinds of meat-roast beef, chicken, salmon, sausages. The smell was heavenly and it was all Izzy could do not to reach out and stuff some into her mouth.

Izzy resisted the pull from the meat table and went past it to the next one. Maybe just some fruit or a dinner roll she thought. The table in front of her was covered with fruit trays and she reached out and picked up an apple slice. As she brought it up to her mouth something caught her eye and she put the apple slice down as she stepped over to the next table. A dessert table! Neatly placed in rows across the white linen tablecloth were dozens of dessert trays. Cake trays, pie trays, stacks of donuts, pyramids of different kinds of cookies, bowls of ice cream, stacks of chocolates, truffles, even a dish of jelly beans!

Izzy turned and slowly looked behind her, first to the right and then to the left. Everyone was busy talking or dancing. She took a plate and placed a small piece of cherry pie on it. Slowly, she cut a small piece off with her fork and lifted it to her mouth. It was like eating for the first time! She quickly finished the pie, set down the plate, and wiped her mouth with a napkin, pleased with her first taste of food in days. Izzy turned to leave but suddenly stopped. It wasn't enough. She thought it would be but she was wrong. The laws of nature were in charge now, not Izzy, and days of starvation couldn't be satisfied by one tiny piece of cherry pie. Almost involuntarily, Izzy reached out, snatched a cookie, and shoved it in her mouth, then grabbed another before she was even done with the first. The cookies were quickly followed by a donut, two truffles, some ice cream, and another donut. Still not satisfied, Izzy swallowed two more cookies and then cut off a huge slab of chocolate cake. Ravenous, she shoved huge fork-fulls of the cake into her mouth, catching the stray pieces with her hands as they fell out the corners of her mouth and pushing them back in. Finally, almost triumphantly, she was finished. She set the empty plate on the table and reached for a napkin.

"Izzy!"

She turned around quickly and stared. "Ghello Chom," Izzy mumbled, her mouth and face still full of chocolate cake.

Tom stared at her as if she were a Martian.

"What's the deal, Izzy?," Tom asked angrily "You walk off and leave me and I have to spend ten minutes looking for you. I finally find you and you're huddled over a table stuffing half-a-pound of chocolate cake down your throat. This ain't cool Izzy!"

Izzy tried to speak but her mouth was filled with a thick slurry of chocolate and sugar. "I'm thorry Chom," she sputtered. "I wath juth hundry."

"Geez Izzy!," Tom groaned. "This is ridiculous. If somebody sees you they'll think we're both a couple of losers. Come on!" Tom grabbed Izzy by the arm and pulled her away from the table. He hustled her past the row of tables to the far wall of the gymnasium and pulled back the curtain. "Go in the girls bathroom and clean up," he said irately as he pushed her through the curtain.

Izzy pushed open the door and fumbled along the wall of the dark bathroom until she found the light switch and then walked over to the sink. She looked into the mirror and understood why Tom was so upset. Her face was smeared with chocolate frosting and cookie crumbs hung from the corners of her mouth. Her upper teeth were covered with a chocolate goo, leaving her with a ridiculous-looking toothless grin, and red filling from the cherry pie was stuck to the tip of her nose. She felt as horrible as she looked. She'd made a fool of herself in front of Tom and had no idea how she was going to fix it. She washed her hands and her face and scrubbed her teeth with her finger. All the sugar she had eaten made her thirsty and she bent over and gulped water from the faucet and then wiped the frosting off the wall and the light switch with some paper towels. After checking herself in the mirror Izzy turned out the light and left the bathroom. She pulled open the curtain and stepped back into the gymnasium.

"I'm so sorry Tom. Please forgive me!" Izzy pleaded. "I don't know what came over me."

"That was crazy Izzy," Tom replied, his voice calmer than before. "I don't know what your deal is but that was really lame and uncool. We're just lucky nobody saw you. That would be bad for both of us." Tom let out a deep breath and looked at Izzy. "Look, let's just forget about it, okay?" he said.

"I'll just tell them you were in the bathroom. Now let's go. We need to get back to the dance."

"Wait Tom," Izzy said as she grabbed his arm. "Give me a minute. I know that was really bad and I'm sorry. But let me make it up to you. I have something that will make you feel better."

Tom looked annoyed. "Izzy, come on," he complained. "Can't this wait? We need to get back. They'll be looking for us."

"It will only take a minute," Izzy protested. "Calm down." She reached inside the belt around her waist and brought out a folded piece of paper. She smiled at Tom and gently squeezed it into his hand. "From your actress to you. I hope you like it."

"Your talking weird again Izzy," Tom said. "What is this?"

"Please," Izzy said, "just read it."

Tom unfolded the piece of paper, read it quickly, and then stuffed it in his pocket. "This is getting too weird for me, Izzy," he said. "What's this all about?"

Izzy was confused. She hadn't expected Tom to react like this to her poem. "I wrote you a poem," she replied softly, hurt by his indifference. "I loved the ones you wrote me and I thought you might like to have one from me."

Tom paused for a moment and stared at Izzy. "Look, Izzy," he finally said. "I don't know what your problem is but this crazy stuff has got to stop. I didn't write you any stupid poems."

Izzy's heart sank. "You didn't?"

"No," Tom replied, "I didn't. I have no idea what you're talking about but right now it doesn't matter. We need to get back to the dance." He grabbed Izzy by the arm and walked back towards the tables. "And Izzy," he said sternly, "no more crazy stuff."

They hurried across the gym and walked over to join Tom's friends near the dance floor. This time Tom remembered to introduce them to Izzy and for a while she made small-talk with a few of them until finally they went back to talking amongst themselves. She stood quietly next to Tom and watched people dance. She really needed a drink but there was no way she was going to wander off again. Ten minutes later a few people in the group walked away across the dance floor. One of them stopped and whispered something in Tom's ear before following the others across the floor and Tom nodded his head in agreement.

Tom turned and looked at Izzy. "Come on," he said as he followed his friends across the floor.

Izzy followed along behind as Tom walked to the far corner of the gymnasium and stopped near his friends. He looked back behind him for a moment and then suddenly grabbed the curtain. He pulled it open, pushed Izzy through as the others followed, and then stepped through the curtain himself, closing it behind him. Someone turned on a small flashlight and they hurried down a hallway.

"We better hurry," Tom whispered to the others. "Here." He reached into his pocket, pulled out a pack of cigarettes, and handed one to each of his friends. Then he turned and held one out towards Izzy. "Here. Take this."

Izzy froze. She hated cigarettes! It was incredibly stupid to inhale smoke, not to mention the fact that it made your breath stink, rotted your teeth, gave you a hacking cough, and caused heart attacks and cancer. Smoking cigarettes was just plain stupid, especially in school. They would be in enormous trouble if they got caught!.

Tom waved the cigarette in front of Izzy's face and pushed it towards her. "Hurry up!," he whispered. "Take it."

Izzy's heart was pounding. She had made a fool of herself tonight and Tom was already mad at her. If she didn't take the cigarette it would embarrass him in front of his friends and he'd really be angry. It must be a test she thought They were testing her to see if she belonged, to see if she was cool. She couldn't disappoint Tom again!

Izzy reached out and grabbed the cigarette. Tom smiled, pulled out a lighter, and lit everyone's cigarettes. Soon a cloud of acrid white smoke floated above their heads and the bitter smell nearly made Izzy sick as her eyes began to water and sting. Slowly, very slowly, she raised the cigarette to her mouth and took a puff. She immediately coughed as the smoke burned her throat but she could tell from Tom's menacing glare that she shouldn't cough again. She took a few more drags and, somewhat painfully, managed to stop the cough before it came out. A few minutes later Tom collected the cigarettes, smashed them against the wall to put them out, and then stuffed the butts back into the package. Tom grabbed Izzy and led her down the hall, stopping at the curtain. The flashlight went out and Izzy was pushed back through the curtain into the gymnasium. Tom stepped out next to her, casually looked around, and then walked out onto the crowded dance floor.

Izzy followed Tom out to the dance floor, her head spinning from the smoke and the confusion.What had gotten into Tom? He had never acted like this before. It didn't make any sense. She wanted to talk to him about it but it was impossible to talk on the dance floor. It was packed with people and it was way too loud. Maybe that's why he came out here she thought.

"Hey Izzy!"

Izzy looked up and saw Cassandra Smithton waving excitedly.

"Hi Izzy," Cassandra yelled as she walked over and hugged her. "You look absolutely fabulous!"

"Thanks Cassandra," Izzy answered. "You look fabulous too!"

"Thanks girlfriend," Cassandra shouted above the music. "Guess what? I talked to the dee-jay and he's going to play "YMCA" right now. Come on girl. Let's dance!"

Cassandra grabbed Izzy's hand and pulled her to the middle of the floor. Tom and a group of other people came out and formed a large circle. Right on cue the pumping beat of "YMCA" blared out from the stereo as everyone began to dance wildly. The tom-tom beat of the music thumped and everyone bounced along with it, throwing their arms in the air to form the letters each time the band sang "Y – M – C –A." Izzy loved the YMCA song and danced along wildly, happy for the chance to enjoy herself and forget for a while everything that had gone wrong. She jumped and spun, she twisted and whirled, throwing her arms high in the air each time the crowd chanted "Y –M –C – A." People all around the circle danced crazily and bodies began bumping together. Izzy joined the frenzy, knocking into other people as she jumped and twisted and pumped her arms.

And then it hit her. She stopped and stood still. She felt like she was twisting and spinning but she wasn't. The warmth came up and her face flushed and she started to sweat as little lights floated across her eyes. She blinked hard but the lights still floated in the air and the room swayed around her. Izzy bent over and put her hands on her knees. She wanted to run but she couldn't move and could hardly think. The days of starvation, the pounds of dessert, the cigarettes and the smoke, the heat and the wild dancing. It was all too much. She tried to stop it but she couldn't. She felt the knot as it formed in her stomach. She felt the spasm as it moved up to her chest. Izzy groaned, fell on her hands and knees, and puked all over the dance floor.

Sometimes The Truth Hurts

It was a beautiful and quiet Sunday morning. The dance hadn't ended until well past midnight and the Exeter campus was nearly deserted as everyone took advantage of the opportunity to sleep late after a long night of partying and dancing. The sun was bright and high and today promised to be the warmest day in weeks. It was only ten-thirty but already a steady drip of melting snow ran from the roofs and puddles of slush pockmarked the sidewalks. A few noisy birds flitted about, happy for the warmth and the puddles, but except for the sound of the birds and the dripping water the campus was completely silent.

Izzy was oblivious to the birds and the water and even to the bright sunshine that filled her room. She lay sprawled across the bed, the covers pulled tightly over her head, with only her right arm visible amongst the jumble of pillows and blankets. A square piece of white tape was stuck to the back of her hand, covering a small bruise where the school nurse had placed the IV line. Another bandage surrounded her elbow and covered the puncture site where the nurse had drawn the blood for the lab tests. After Izzy vomited all over the gym floor Mr. Crandall and another teacher had taken her to the school infirmary. The nurse was so concerned by Izzy's condition that she drew blood for lab tests and found that Izzy was severely dehydrated and dangerously low on potassium because of her starvation diet. She started an IV line and Izzy lay on a bed for three hours while two liters of saline dripped into her vein. She also got two shots, one in her arm and one in her butt, for anti-nausea medication but she had been too delirious to feel them. Because of her delirium she had no way of knowing that Principal Thompkins, as well as her parents, were notified of her condition. And she wouldn't remember that it was Angela that had cared for her last night, Angela that put cool washclothes on her pounding head and rubbed her back and emptied the trash can each time she threw up.

Izzy opened her eyes and pulled the covers off her head as she rolled onto her back. Her head still hurt but the horrible throbbing that had tortured her all night was gone. Her mouth was as dry as dirt and her teeth were covered in a thin film of old sugar. She sat up in bed and leaned back against the headboard. Memories of last night slowly came into focus except for the jumbled mess of thoughts and dreams about what happened after the dance. She studied the bandages on her arm and could remember being in the nurse's office but what had happened there was lost in a stuporous fog.

Izzy slid her legs over the side of the bed and carefully stood up. She picked up the bottle of water on the nightstand and gulped down half of it, waited for a moment, and then drank the rest. The water made her feel better almost immediately and helped to clear her head as well as her mouth. She squinted at the brightness in the room and slowly looked around. Angela was gone and the room was neat and clean like it usually was. Izzy walked slowly over to her armoire and pulled back the doors. Her black dress had been cleaned and hung neatly on a hangar and her shoes were in place on the second shelf.

A terrible thought slowly crept into Izzy's mind and she closed the armoire. She went over to Angela's armoire, opened it and gently pulled out the jewelry box. Please, please! Haltingly, she pulled back the lid, and looked inside, and then let out a sigh of relief. Angela's necklace, the one her mother had given her, was in it's place and so were the watch and bracelets Izzy had worn last night.

Izzy carefully put the jewelry box back on the shelf and closed the armoire. Last night had been bad enough and she was relieved that she didn't have another problem to deal with. She grabbed some clothes and her shower bag and headed down the hall to the bathroom. The hallway and the bathroom were quiet and empty and she was glad for that. She wasn't ready to deal with the laughing and the questions and the stares. She stepped into the shower and turned the water to full hot, hopeful that the warmth would soothe her aching muscles. She stayed in the shower for twenty minutes and washed her hair three times before the stench of vomit and smoke was finally gone. The shower revived her and her body aches were gone and she almost felt normal. When she was done she grabbed her shower bag and walked back down the empty hall to her room.

Izzy closed the door behind her and dropped the bag on the floor. She was really hungry and the dining room would be open in five minutes. The lesson had been learned and the starvation diet was over.

Izzy walked to her desk and slid open the drawer to get her lunch card but as she reached out to grab it her hand suddenly stopped and Izzy froze. She took a step backwards and covered her mouth with her hands.

No! It can't be! Lying next to her lunch card was a small white envelope neatly addressed to "Miss Isabella Watson." Her hands trembled as she reached into the drawer, picked up the envelope, and opened it.

The World Will Bring Trouble And Pain.
Walk In It And Receive The Stain
For It Can Take The Strong And Bold
And Leave Them All Weak And Cold
Stand Alone And Accept Your Fate
Or Run Toward The Narrow Gate
Only Love Can Conquer All
At Its' Feet The World Will Fall
Use The Power Inside The Heart
From The One Who Stands Apart
If You Wish Troubles To Cease
Claim The Crown That Brings You Peace

Izzy stared down at the letter, dumbfounded. How could this be? Who could this be? Tom had certainly made it clear last night that he wasn't the one writing the poems. But if it wasn't Tom, who was it? Izzy studied the poem's meaning. The first part made perfect sense-"The world will bring trouble and pain." She had certainly seen that firsthand last night. The rest of the poem suggested that the only thing a person has to fight the world with is love, though that seemed to Izzy to be a strange thing to fight with. Maybe this was another love note, maybe there was someone else out there that was in love with her. But who?

Izzy's mind spun aimlessly as it chased dozens of questions down dozens of paths, none leading to any answers. Finally, she gave up in frustration and put the letter back in the drawer. It was all too much and too confusing and she was so hungry and weak she couldn't think straight. Maybe after she got something to eat her mind could calm down and focus enough that she could make sense of all of it. She picked up the lunch pass and closed the drawer. Quickly, she stepped into her shoes, grabbed her jacket, and headed out the door.

The hallway was still empty and quiet but as Izzy walked down the stairs she could see a few people standing in the atrium. No one spoke to her as she walked by nor did anyone say anything as she made her way through the lunch line. She loaded her tray down with roast beef, green beans, dinner rolls, and salad but, remembering the events of last night, she decided to put half of it back. Izzy swiped her card across the cash register and walked over to a table in the corner beneath the large windows. The food smelled really good and she was starving but she forced herself to slow down and eat slowly. Her stomach was still upset and she didn't want a replay of last night, ever. She took a few small bites, stared out the window for awhile, and then cautiously took a few more bites. As she slowly chewed her food and gazed absent-mindedly out the window something caught her eye. From where she sat Izzy could see almost the entire courtyard, nearly all the way over to the library. Two people were walking along the sidewalk holding hands, a tall boy in a red jacket and a dark-haired girl in jeans and a blue coat. Izzy turned away. Seeing them only made her think of Tom and after last night she wasn't sure whether she had a boyfriend anymore. She took a few more bites and tried not to look outside but there was nothing else to look at and her eyes naturally went back to the two sweethearts. Izzy followed them as they strolled along the sidewalk towards her.

"No!," Izzy cried outloud. "It can't be!" She leaned forward and peered through the window. The two sweethearts stopped under a tree fifty feet from where Izzy sat staring at them. The tall boy gently pushed the girl's hair back with his hand, pulled her tightly against him, and kissed her.

Tom! Izzy's jaw clenched and she nearly bent the fork she held in her hand. From where she sat she could clearly see Tom Andrews as he held the dark-haired girl close to him. Finally, they pulled apart and Izzy could see the girl's face. It was Susan Morris, Cassandra's faithful sidekick and best friend! Izzy forced herself to look away. How could he do this to me? It was cruel and mean and embarrassing! Izzy was stunned and hurt and stared blankly down at the table in front of her. The "hows" and the "why's" whirled in her head but after a few minutes they didn't matter anymore. Izzy was mad!

She pushed the food away from her and stood up. Someone said "Hello" as she stormed out of the dining room but Izzy never heard it as she headed for the door. The doors flew open ahead of her and she marched quickly down the steps, turning left at the bottom as she strode down the sidewalk toward Tom and Susan Morris. Tom leaned in and kissed Susan again and she turned and walked up the sidewalk in the opposite direction. Tom stood and watched her walk away, waved, and turned around.

"Would you like to explain that Tom?," Izzy said angrily, inches from his face and her right hand clenched in a fist.

"Uh, I, uh," Tom stammered as a look of shock and fear spread cross his face. "Look Izzy, I…."

"You what?," Izzy yelled. "I was sick and you got so lonely that you just had to make-out with Susan Morris? Nice Tom, real nice!"

"That's not it Izzy," he protested. "I was going to come and talk to you. I was."

"To say what?," Izzy growled.

Tom stared passively at the ground. "To say that it's over," he answered.

Izzy was too angry to fully feel the hurt of what Tom said. Obviously it was over! He hardly needed to tell her that. Izzy wanted more. "I know it's over Tom," Izzy said caustically. "I kind of figured that out when I saw you swapping spit with Susan. What I want to know is why? I think I deserve an explanation. Is this because of last night?"

Tom's shoulders slumped and he sighed. "That's part of it Izzy," he answered. "You've got to admit that what you did was really lame and embarrassing. People made fun of me all night!"

"So," Izzy replied coldly, "I embarrassed you in front of your hot-shot friends so you dump me. I guess you have to protect your image and your reputation, huh?"

"That's part of it, yea," Tom answered weakly. "But it really doesn't matter now."

"What do you mean by "part of it," Izzy asked. "There's more?"

"Ah, come on Izzy," Tom said, "let it go. It's over."

Tom apparently didn't know about Izzy's temper. She'd had enough of his whimpering! She reached out and grabbed the front of Tom's jacket. "Look buddy," she said as she twisted the jacket in her fist, "you're going to get a knee right where you don't want one if you don't tell me the truth. I'll leave you laying on the sidewalk crying. What would your big shot friends think of you then?"

Tom's eyes were wide-open and he stared at Izzy. "Izzy, come on, I don't….."

"Now Andrews!," Izzy yelled.

"Fine, okay," Tom said. Izzy let go of his jacket and stood stiffly in front of him. "If you really want to hear it I'll tell you the truth."

"All of it," Izzy said.

"Are you sure you…."

"Now!," Izzy snapped.

"Okay," Tom said. "Calm down. One reason I'm breaking up with you is about last night. Another reason is because I know your secret."

Izzy stared at him. "What secret?"

"You know, that you're adopted and not really a Watson," Tom replied.

Izzy paused for a moment and wondered how Tom knew about the adoption. "What's that got to do with anything?," Izzy asked. "And how do you know about it?"

"Well," Tom began, "Cassandra told me that you were adopted. How she knows I have no idea. As to why it matters, well, it's like this. Part of the reason I went out with you was because you were a Watson. I told you, the Watson name is like royalty at Exeter and dating a Watson means something. It makes you cool and gives you instant status, kind of like if you date Brittney Spears or Jennifer Lopez. But, if you aren't really a Watson well, you know, that means it's not quite as big a deal to go out with you."

Tom's words stung Izzy in the heart. She wanted to cry but wasn't about to let that happen. A few tears started to come but she squeezed them out of her eyes and glared at Tom. "Silly me," she said calmly, "I thought you wanted to go out with me, not my name."

"Well," Tom answered hesitantly, "that was part of the deal."

Izzy scowled at Tom. "Deal?," she said, "What deal?"

Tom fidgeted, obviously sorry that he had let the words come out of his mouth. "The deal I made with Cassandra," Tom answered. "If you really want to know the truth, here it is. I really wanted to go out with Susan Morris all along. Cassandra is her best friend and she said she would set me up with Susan if I did her a favor. She wanted me to go out with you and try to find some dirt on you, you know, something embarrassing. I figured it was a good deal for me. I got to go out with a Waston, which would make me look good, and then Cassandra would hook me up with Susan. And Cassandra had a plan that we would build you up, you know, make you cool and popular, and then Cassandra could bring you down. She's still furious about the snake you put in her locker. But then I got to know you and found out you were really cool. I tried to get out of the deal but Cassandra threatened me. She said she had a lot of stuff on me and would ruin me if I backed out and I'd never get to go out with Susan. I'm really sorry Izzy. I didn't want it to end like this. I really didn't."

Izzy tried to swallow the lump in her throat but it wouldn't go away. She stiffened as the pain and the hurt washed over her like a wave. It was hard to believe the ruthlessness, the utter cruelty, of Cassandra Smithton. "So," Izzy said softly, "this was all a lie, some kind of sick game?"

"Something like that," Tom answered. "High school can be that way Izzy."

Izzy stared at Tom but there was nothing left to say. She turned around, took a few steps, and then ran towards Franklin Hall as the tears streamed down her face.

****

Izzy walked down the hallway towards the girls bathroom to get ready for school. Physically she felt much better. The headaches were gone, her appetite was back to normal, and the bruise on her right hand no long hurt. But emotionally

Izzy was a mess. It has often been said that your first broken heart hurts the worst and Izzy was just the latest to prove the old saying true. She had cried most of the day yesterday and into the night. For some reason Angela was gone and Izzy had spent the day and the long night alone and miserable. She ached for someone to talk to, for someone to comfort her and tell her everything would be alright. But no one was there. Not Angela or Link or Iam or Gabriel or her parents. No one. The loneliness only made her pain more bitter.

Izzy walked into the bathroom, set her bag and her clothes on the bench, and stepped into the shower. A few other girls were in the bathroom but they hadn't said anything to Izzy when she came in but now Izzy could hear them talking and laughing. She finished her shower, wrapped a towel around her body and another around her head, and walked over to the sink. She heard the other girls start to giggle and could now plainly see the reason for their laughter. Taped to the mirror was a piece of paper, the poem she had written and given to Tom at the dance Saturday night.

> *I know how much you love poetry so I thought I would try to write you one. Hope you like it! Hugs and Kisses from your actress. Izzy*

You Own My Heart, You Know It's True
There Are No Others, Only You
Dashing, Handsome, A Perfect Face
You Send My Heart To Outer Space!
You Smile At Me And I Nearly Melt
It's Like Nothing Else I Ever Felt
There Is No Doubt You Came From Above
A Gift To Me, For Me To Love

Izzy's muscles tightened and she tried to ignore the muffled laughter behind her. She had expected more trouble from Cassandra Smithton so seeing the poem posted in the girls bathroom wasn't a surprise. What surprised her and what really hurt was that Tom had given it to Cassandra. Apparently it was worth it to humiliate her in order to get a date with Susan Morris. Unwilling to supply the bathroom queens with the tearful drama they hoped to see, Izzy ignored the poem. She knew they were waiting for her to breakdown, to tear the poem off the mirror while she sobbed and wailed. But that wasn't going to happen. She wouldn't give them or Cassandra the satisfaction.

Izzy calmly brushed her teeth and then worked quickly on her hair, blow drying it and pulling it back in a ponytail. She put on her uniform and her shoes and stuffed her belongings into the shower bag. The hushed giggling had stopped but Izzy could feel that she was still being watched. She flung the shower bag over her shoulder, straightened her uniform, and walked toward the door.

"Hey Watson!" Cassandra Smithton stood near the bathroom door, leaning casually against the wall while Susan Morris and two of her other puppets blocked the doorway.

"Is your tummy feeling better?," Cassandra said mockingly as if she were talking to a baby.

"I'm fine," Izzy answered stiffly.

"That's nice," Cassandra purred. "The girls and I were so afraid your little tummy-ache would turn into a dreadful spasm of diarrhea." The puppets roared with obedient laughter.

Izzy tightened but she didn't move as a circle of girls formed around her, everyone wanting to watch as the great Cassandra Smithton closed in on her prey.

"You poor dear," Cassandra said as she slowly shook her head from side to side, "You've had a terrible couple of days, haven't you? What an awful shame." She stepped away from the wall and circled Izzy like a spider walking her web. "You lost your dinner all over the gym floor, lost your boyfriend to another woman, and now this!" She snatched the poem off the mirror and shoved it towards Izzy. "Now you've lost whatever shred of dignity you had left!"

The room was completely quiet. Izzy still hadn't moved and glared icily at Cassandra. "I'll survive," she replied confidently.

"Marvellous!," Cassandra exclaimed. "I'm happy to see that you are so strong and emotionally balanced. Because there is just one more little issue we need to discuss. It's a pity too. I hate to do it since you've lost so much already. But I'm afraid I must. I need to inform you that you are no longer a member of the cheerleading squad."

Izzy nearly laughed. Did Cassandra really think she cared about being on the cheerleading team?

"Why are you kicking me off the team?," Izzy asked, though the reason didn't particularly matter to her.

"Why?," Cassandra exclaimed. "How about embarrassing the entire cheerleading squad? Cheerleaders do not vomit on the floor in the middle of a school dance! It's classless and shows extremely poor taste. And getting dumped by your boyfriend? That is completely unacceptable. We dump them, they never dump us. Nobody dumps a cheerleader."

Cassandra again started to circle Izzy and the other girls backed away as she closed in. "But wait! There's more. How about writing juvenile, syrupy, and just plain awful poetry? That just perpetuates the myth that cheerleaders aren't intelligent, that we are just beautiful and talented air-heads. In short, you are a disgrace to cheerleaders Watson and......Wait!"

Cassandra stopped in mid-sentence and raised her finger in the air. She leaned back against the sink, folded her arms, and smiled. "I nearly forgot," she said. "There's one more reason to kick you off the team. You lied on your application."

"I did not!," Izzy scowled.

"I'm afraid you did," Cassandra replied slyly. "You gave your name as Izzy Watson. But you aren't Izzy Watson. You're no Watson at all. You're adopted!"

Izzy heard the circle of girls gasp and then begin to murmer. To them a name meant something. To them, a famous name was a badge of honor, an image maker, a status symbol.

"I may be adopted but so what?," Izzy replied angrily. "My name is still Izzy Watson. And I am a member of the Watson family."

Cassandra laughed. "And I'm a Kennedy!," she cried. "You're no more a Watson than the man on the moon. To be a Watson at Exeter, a real Watson, means something. But to be a fake Watson means nothing. And to pretend to be a Watson is scandalous and pathetic. Did you really think it would work? Did you really think you could be one of us?"

Izzy began to tremble. Her anger had kept her from falling apart but Cassandra's final hammer-stroke was too much. Tears welled-up in her eyes and slowly spilled down her face. Without the adrenaline rush of her anger she felt beaten and weak, unable even to attempt a defense. Her chin fell to her chest and the soft sound of sobbing echoed through the quiet bathroom. Cassandra stood triumphantly at the sink, an arrogant , self – important smirk across her face. But the other girls, even the puppets, wore uncomfortable looks of pain on their faces as they listened to Izzy sob.

Finally, Izzy stopped. She shifted the bag on her shoulder, stood up straight, and wiped the tears from her face. Izzy was done, done with the self-pity and the guilt, done with the anger and the anguish, done with the lies and the drama. Her world for the last two days had been nothing but hurt and pain but now something deep inside her said "Enough!" But this was no voice of surrender and submission that spoke to Izzy. It did not speak from weakness or defeat and did not ask for mercy. No, this voice spoke with power, a power that came from an awakening of the old Izzy, from the strong and self-confident

Izzy that existed before high-school turned her life into a soap opera.

Izzy turned her head and scanned the circle of girls surrounding her. She looked each one of them squarely in the eye but they all turned away, unable to withstand the intensity of her stare. They had thought Izzy was beaten but she wasn't, and they knew it, and they slowly backed away. Izzy turned and looked directly at Cassandra. The confident smirk she wore slowly faded as now even Cassandra could sense that something had changed. A confused look of near panic came across her face, as when the hunter becomes the hunted, and Cassandra slowly slid away from Izzy toward her friends. Izzy took a step forward, the circle of girls parted, and she walked out of the bathroom.

Izzy stopped in the hallway and looked at her watch. She only had five minutes before she needed to leave for class. She didn't have time for breakfast but that didn't matter. The confrontation with Cassandra had spoiled her appetite and the dining room would just stir up bad memories. Instead, she dropped her shower bag off in her room, grabbed her jacket, and headed for class. As she walked downstairs one of the teachers greated her with a polite "Good Morning." Izzy smiled and returned the greeting. It wasn't until she was outside on the sidewalk that she realized that she had smiled again, even if it was only a polite smile, and it made Izzy feel better. Maybe things actually would get better and she would make it through her freshman year of high school.

Izzy walked up the steps into Graham Hall and then turned left and walked down the hallway. She rounded the corner and headed to her locker, arriving there at precisely the same moment as Principal Thompkins.

"Good morning Miss Watson," the Principal said sternly.

"Good morning ma'am," Izzy answered politely.

"Would you kindly open your locker Miss Watson," the Principal said.

"Why?," Izzy asked, confused by her request.

"Miss Watson!," Principal Thompkins exclaimed. "I shall ask the questions here. Please do as you are told."

Izzy was completely confused but she knew better than to do anything else but obey. Nervously, she spun the dial on the lock, removed it, and swung open the locker door. Principal Thompkins stepped forward, pushed Izzy to the side, and pulled a large manila envelope out of the locker.

"What is this doing in your locker?," she said accusingly.

"What is it?," Izzy asked, clueless as to what was happening.

Principal Thompkins hovered over Izzy, her large square jaw clenched as she jabbed the folder in the air inches from Izzy's face. "I did not come here to play twenty questions Miss Watson!," she fumed. "I came here for answers not for questions. You are in terrible trouble young lady and your disagreeable attitude will only make matters worse."

Izzy was stunned. She had no idea what Principal Thompkins was talking about! She tried to collect her thoughts but it was impossible when she had no clue what was happening. The hulking figure of the Principal glowering down at her only made the situation worse. Izzy started to mumble a reply but was drowned out by the sound of the first class bell. Students quickly filled the hallway but their usual boisterous chatter ceased immediately when they saw Principal Thompkins. Several students offered a polite "Good morning Ma'am" as they walked by but most simply dropped their heads and scurried past.

Izzy was thankful for the brief pause in Principal Thompkins attack. At the moment, the Principal's attention was diverted as she greeted the passing students and she was no longer looking at Izzy. The manila folder was in her left hand and Izzy craned her neck up and down as she tried to get a look at it. But the Principal's claw-like hand covered half the folder and it moved each time the Principal moved until finally it disappeared behind her back. Desperate for a clue as to what was happening Izzy cautiously stepped to the right and leaned in as she tried to get a glimpse of the folder. But it was no use. The folder was firmly pressed against the Principal's back and Izzy couldn't see it. But she saw something else. Standing near the doorway of the English room was Cassandra Smithton and two giggling side-kicks. Cassandra looked at Izzy, smirked, and silently mouthed "Have a nice day. Loser!"

The final class bell rang and Principal Thompkins immediately renewed the assault. "Now Miss Watson," she said calmly, "where were we? Ah, yes. You were about to explain to me how a copy of today's geometry test came to be in your locker."

Izzy's eyes got huge. The geometry test! She didn't even know she had a geometry test today. With everything that had happened over the weekend it had completely slipped her mind. And she obviously had no idea how a copy of the test had gotten in her locker. "Mrs. Thompkins," Izzy sputtered. "I have no idea….."

"Come now Isabella!," the Principal exclaimed. "Do not play me for a fool! A copy of the test with all the answers on it is found in your locker and you have no idea how it got there? You are trying my patience young lady."

"Honest Mrs. Thompkins!," Izzy protested. "I've never seen that folder before and I didn't take it."

Principal Thompkins took in a deep breath and then slowly exhaled. "For the sake of argument," she said calmly, "let's pretend that what you say is true. You did not take the test but it very clearly was in your locker. Thus, it must follow logically that someone else stole the test and then that certain someone placed the test in your locker. Is that your story, Miss Watson?"

Someone else? The thought of it nearly took her breath away as the answer hit Izzy solidly in the gut. Cassandra! The meanness and cruelty of it almost made her cry.

"Miss Watson!," the Principal barked, bringing Izzy back from her thoughts. "Is that your story, that someone else put the test in your locker?"

"I guess," Izzy answered weakly.

"Well then," the Principal replied, "please tell me who else has the combination to your locker."

Izzy swallowed hard. "No one."

"Well, that certainly doesn't support your story, does it?," the Principal replied. "Perhaps you would like to try some other defense. Do you have an alibi?"

"A what?," Izzy asked.

"An alibi Miss Watson," the Principal remarked calmly as she closed in for the kill. "From the Latin "alius ibi," meaning that the accused can show that they were not present at the time and place of the crime."

Izzy felt the noose loosen. She had an alibi! "When was the test stolen?," she asked quickly.

"This morning," the Principal replied, "between seven and eight o'clock."

Izzy brightened. "I was in the girls bathroom," she answered confidently.

Principal Thompkins shook her head slowly and sighed. "I was afraid of that," she replied. "I have already questioned Cassandra Smithton and several of the other girls Isabella. They have told me that no one saw you in the girls bathroom this morning."

The trap was sprung. Cassandra had thought of everything. Izzy had no proof, no excuse, no alibi, and now she had no escape. It was finally over. Cassandra had won and Izzy had lost.

"Excuse me, Principal Thompkins."

Izzy and the Principal turned around. Angela limped up to where they were standing and stopped in front of Principal Thompkins.

"I'm sorry to interrupt," Angela said politely, "but I need to speak with you."

"Who might you be?," the Principal asked as she glared at Angela.

"I am Angela Wagner," she replied. "I am a friend of Isabella's."

"Forgive me for forgetting your name," the Principal answered. "I was a bit distracted. Miss Watson and I are having a conversation. I shall speak to you at some later time."

Angela didn't move. "I know the seriousness of your conversation with Isabella and I believe I can help," she said.

The Principal paused for a moment, a confused look on her face. "Speak!," she said sharply.

"I am the one who took the test," Angela said calmly.

Principal Thompkins and Izzy both stepped backward as if Angela had pushed them, stunned by what they had just heard. Izzy's mind whirled in confusion. What was Angela doing? Is she crazy? Stealing a test meant getting expelled from school! Izzy knew there as no way Angela had stolen the test. Angela had a 99.6 % average in geometry! She didn't need to steal the test.

Principal Thompkins regained her composure and held the folder out towards Angela. "You stole this test and put it in Miss Watson's locker?," she asked.

"I did," Angela answered firmly. "I did not mean for Isabella to get involved. But someone came down the hall and I panicked. I needed somewhere to hide the test so I put it in the locker."

Principal Thompkins reached out, shut the locker door, and fastened the lock. She stepped to the side and motioned Angela toward the locker. Angela calmly walked over and grabbed the lock. She spun the dial to the right, back to the left, and finally to the right again. She removed the lock and swung open the door.

"Principal Thompkins, there's no way......"

"Quiet Miss Watson!," the Principal said firmly. "I believe the issue has been settled." She turned to face Izzy and put her hand on Izzy's shoulder. "I owe you an apology Isabella," she said politely. "Forgive me for not believing you. I'm sure you will agree that all of the evidence pointed to your guilt. But I was mistaken and you have my deepest and most sincere apology. You may go now. Miss Wagner and I will be leaving as well."

Principal Thompkins took Angela by the arm and began to walk away down the hall. Izzy stood quietly, dazed and completely dumbfounded by what had just happened. She watched as they walked down the hall and then turned to go around the corner. As they rounded the corner Angela turned and looked back over her shoulder. Her face broke into a bright smile and she winked at Izzy.

Finally, Answers

The week had been unseasonably warm. The thaw started the day after the Christmas Dance and the days had gotten steadily warmer ever since. The older people, even Principal Thompkins, had never seen anything like it. For nearly a month the entire Exeter campus had been covered in snow but now not a single flake remained, not even in the shade under the big oaks. Instead of snow and ice the campus was instead covered in the heat of a bright sunshine that pushed the thermometer past seventy degrees.

Izzy could feel the heat of the morning sun as she stood next to the window in her pajamas. She stretched her arms over her head and arched her back as she squeezed her eyes shut tightly and tried to push the sleep from her head. She had planned to sleep late this morning but the brightness and heat of the room made sleeping uncomfortable and impossible. The room was quiet, like it had been all week. Angela was gone and the room seemed to miss her as much as Izzy did. Even with the warmth and the sunshine pouring through the window the room still felt empty and cold. It was like a jail cell and it needed to change.

Izzy walked over to the armoire, knelt down, and opened the bottom drawer. She pulled out the shoebox and dumped the contents on the floor beside her. Out spilled all of the decorations that she had previously hung around the room to give the room color and character. She grabbed several pairs of colorful socks and two strings of glass beads and strung them along the coat rack on the back of the door. Not satisfied, she took some feathers and hung them from the edge of the lamp shade and wrapped the lamp cord with a canary yellow scarf. She tied a few socks and some multi-colored handkerchiefs together to make a garland and wrapped it through the wooden slots on the back of her desk chair, and then stepped back to admire her work. It looked better but she could tell that something was missing. She closed her eyes and tried to picture what the room had looked like before. Suddenly, the thought hit her and she opened her eyes.

Izzy walked over to Angela's armoire, took a slow breath, and pulled open the doors. Sitting alone on the empty shelf was a shoebox. Izzy picked up the box and sat down on the floor, amazed by Angela's kindness and compassion. She lifted off the lid and stared at the jewelry. In her head Izzy could hear the caustic words she had said to Angela as she shoved the box at her and demanded that she take it. And she could hear Angela's gentle reply – "Oh Izzy! This is all of your favorite jewelry. You made these things yourself. I can't take this!" Izzy shuddered at the thought of herself but smiled at the memory of Angela.

Izzy got up and put the box on her desk. She took the larger necklaces and hung them around the posts of the beds and draped others across the window where they could sparkle in the sun. Her favorite necklace, the blue one with the red beads and the leather and the feathers, she placed around her neck.

She put the rest of the jewelry on the shelf in her armoire and then pulled open the drawer. From the very bottom of the drawer she retrieved a pair of pants, a pair she hadn't seen or worn in four months. They were white and one leg had been split to the knee. Into the split was sewn a triangular piece of denim with yellow stars across it. Izzy put on the pants and then slipped a red sneaker onto her right foot and a yellow sneaker onto her left. From the bottom of a stack of shirts she pulled a red and blue striped blouse, which she put on and left un-tucked, and covered it with a denim vest. She tied a red handkerchief around her neck and a thin leather strap across her forehead. When she finished tying the strap Izzy stopped and looked in the mirror, staring at the reflection of an old friend.

It was too nice a day to stay inside and after doing a few things around the room Izzy left and headed outside. She walked out of Franklin Hall and turned up the sidewalk towards the library at the far end of the campus. A lot of students were already outside in the courtyard enjoying the weather, some reading or laying in the sun and others playing Frisbee over in the far corner. Izzy stayed on the sidewalk until she was close to the library and then turned and walked across the brown grass towards the fence a hundred yards away. When she reached the fence Izzy stopped and looked behind her. She couldn't see anyone so she opened the gate and stepped through, closing it tightly behind her. She ran down the path until she was out of sight near the river and then slowed to a walk. Even in the thick forest along the river the air was warm and the occasional small pile of snow was the only reminder that it was still winter. Izzy walked slowly along the trail, pausing occasionally to admire the view and to warm her face in the sun. The trail broke to the left up the hill and she followed it to the top where she found Iam's woodpile but nothing else. She stood still and listened, hoping to hear the sound of a dog barking, but she heard nothing and continued up the trail as it zig-zagged through the woods.

After a few minutes she crossed the wooden bridge and saw the cabin ahead of her through the trees. Finally, she heard the familiar bark and ran towards it.

"Gabriel!," Izzy shouted as she fell to her knees. Gabriel ran through the trees and jumped into her arms, his tail wagging wildly as he licked her face.

"I missed you boy!," Izzy said as she hugged his neck. "I really did!" She tried to stand up but in his excitement Gabriel knocked her to the ground. Izzy laughed and pushed him away as she got up.

"That's enough you silly boy!," Izzy laughed. "Is Iam here Gabriel?"

Gabriel barked and ran to the porch. He sat down at the bottom of the steps and barked again. Izzy followed him up the gravel path and as she approached the cabin she saw Iam come out of the house. He sat down on the top step while Izzy took a seat on the bottom step next to Gabriel.

"Hi Iam," Izzy said.

"Good morning, Isabella," Iam replied with a smile. "Gabriel and I are glad to see you."

Izzy looked down and petted Gabriel. "I know he's glad to see me," she said softly, "I just hope that you are too."

"Come now Isabella," Iam answered, "friends can't let a few angry words come between them, can they?"

"You're not mad at me?," Izzy replied hopefully.

"Of course not Isabella," he laughed. "Friends don't stay mad at each other very long. You will find that Gabriel and I are a lot alike, very loyal and forgiving."

Izzy smiled at Iam as she scratched Gabriel's ears. "I suppose you heard about what happened," she said.

"Indeed, yes I have," Iam said. "A terrible thing, most dreadful. Are you alright?"

Izzy leaned back against the railing and rested her arm on her knee. "Yea, I'm okay," she answered. "It's getting better. But I don't want to talk about that stuff. I came to ask you a favor."

"Of course," Iam replied. "I am in the favor business. Gabriel and I are at your service."

Izzy stood up, reached into her back pocket, and pulled out some folded sheets of paper. "It's a long story," she said, "but I was hoping you could read these poems and help me figure out what they mean." She handed the papers to Iam and sat back down on the step. He unfolded them slowly and carefully read each one. When he was finished he folded the papers and handed them back to Izzy.

"Shall we start with the first one?," Iam asked.

"Sure," Izzy responded. She shuffled the sheets and looked at the first poem.

See Not The Air That Gives You Breath
Yet Without It Certain Death
You Pass It By But Do Not See
Does That Mean It Cannot Be?
The Desert Boy He Sees Not Snow
Does That Mean No Blizzards Blow?
How Many Things The Hand Can't Feel
This Does Not Mean They Are Not Real
You Cannot See If You Close Your Eyes
Open Them If You Wish Be Wise

"This poem seems to be the clearest of the four," Iam began. "The writer first gives examples of things that are quite real even if they are not seen. For example, you cannot see the air that you breath though of course it is obviously there. And just because the young boy was born in a desert and has never seen snow does not mean that snow does not exist. But the most important lines are the last. The author asks you to open your eyes so that you can see, though I think "eyes" and "see" have more than their normal meanings. The eyes are not the only way for a person to observe or to become aware of things. The heart and the mind do the same thing. "If you wish be wise" you must open your heart and your mind as well as your eyes so that you can truly "see." You do not always have to see to believe Isabella."

Izzy sat quietly for a moment and let Iam's words sink in. "I got it!," she said excitedly. "I didn't before but I understand it now. Try the next one Iam." Izzy shuffled the papers and turned to the second poem.

The Age-Old Battle Rages On
The Evil One Is Never Gone
A Roaring Lion Is On The Prowl
Do Not Run When You Hear His Growl
Stand Tall Upon The Primal Stone
Remember That You Are Not Alone
Use The Strength That Lasts Forever
The Hands Have Power When Put Together
The Old Ones Speak An Ancient Tongue
Use Their Words To Fight This One

This poem has many more layers than the first poem," Iam said. "The "Age-Old Battle" represents the battle between good and evil. The "evil one" and the "roaring lion" are one and the same.They represent the devil. To fight this battle you will need help and the author reminds you that you are not alone in this fight. You have many weapons. The "Primal Stone" is faith, which is quite powerful. It is "the strength that lasts forever." You also have the power of "hands put together." This has two meanings. The first is a reminder to reach out and join hands with your family and with your friends.When trouble comes you can use their strength to help you. The other meaning of the hands joined together is prayer, which is a very powerful weapon indeed. The last two lines speak of "Old Ones" and an "Ancient Tongue." This represents the Hebrew, Latin, and Greek languages, which are the original languages of the Bible. The words of the Bible can help you whenever evil crosses your path."

Izzy was amazed at Iam's clear explanation of the poem. She could now understand what it meant though she still had no idea who had written it. "You're really good at this," Izzy said. "Did you study poetry or something?"

Iam laughed. "Something like that," he replied. "They say poetry is music written with words. I have never been very good with music but when the melody is written down I can follow it quite easily."

Izzy smiled. "Can you do the third one for me?," she asked hopefully.

"Of course Isabella," Iam replied.

Izzy pulled out the third poem.

All The World Is Indeed A Stage
It Has Not Changed From Age To Age
The Actress Comes To Play Her Part
Yet Often Leaves A Broken Heart
She Lives Inside What Is Not Real
And Loves The Things That Cannot Heal
The Heart Belongs To The One Above
He Is The One Who Deserves Your Love
You Must Act In A Different Play
One That Lasts Beyond This Day
It Has All That You Desire
Play The Part And Escape The Fire

"The third poem starts with a line borrowed from one of Shakespeare's plays," Iam began. "Life is theater, a play with many acts and scenes. A girl, an "actress," is born and she acts in this theater of life but often times she "leaves the stage," she dies, unhappy and unfulfilled. The reason for her unhappiness is that she has spent her time on stage, her life, chasing after things that have no real value, things like money and fame and power. She forgets to seek after the things that really matter, the things that can heal her empty heart, and the author reminds her that her heart, and her love, belong to "The One Above," that is, to God. The last lines of the poem speak of a "different play," an alternative to a life of emptiness and despair. She is told to act in a different play, an "eternal play," in the theater above where she will find everything she desires. If she does, if she "plays the part," she will escape "the fire," which of course is a symbol of hell."

Izzy was stunned! What she had thought was a love poem from Tom Andrews was instead something altogether different. This was no love letter, it was a sermon, a call to turn her back on the shallow materialism and image-making of life, of high school, and go down a different path. Her mind reeled at the poem's meaning and Iam's answers only led to more questions. Who would write her such a poem? And why?

"Is something wrong Isabella?" Iam asked.

"Well, I, um," Izzy stammered as she collected her thoughts, "I just thought it meant something else, that's all."

"That's understandable," Iam replied. "Many people look at such things and see many different things. Some see a myth or a legend, some simply laugh and turn away, but some see truth and understand."

Izzy shrugged and pulled out the fourth poem. Her mind was too jumbled to understand Iam's words and she wanted to move on to the fourth poem. "Let's try the last one Iam," she said as she looked at the last poem.

The World Will Bring Trouble And Pain
Walk In It And Receive The Stain
For It Can Take The Strong And Bold
And Leave Them All Weak And Cold
Stand Alone And Accept Your Fate
Or Walk Toward The Narrow Gate
Only Love Can Conquer All

At It's Feet The World Will Fall
Use The Power Inside The Heart
From The One Who Stands Apart
If You Wish Troubles To Cease
Claim The Crown That Brings You Peace

"The fourth poem picks up where the third poem left off," Iam said. "Again it points out that in this world you will have troubles. And since we walk in this fallen and afflicted world we are bound to stumble occasionally and acquire "the stain," that is, sin. It happens to everyone no matter how strong they may be. If you try to make it through this world alone you will fail and then you must accept your fate because you have made your decision. Instead, the writer wants you to look toward "the narrow gate," the gate that leads to God, or as the author calls Him "the one who stands apart." For it is there that you will find the only thing that can save you from the world, namely the love that He gives freely. But everyone has a decision to make. If you want your troubles to end you must "claim the crown," meaning you must decide."

Izzy sat silently. Iam had explained the poems clearly and beautifully. She now knew what the words meant though she still didn't understand what the poems meant. They were wonderful poems about life and love and God but what were they telling her? What was she supposed to do now that she knew what they meant? And the ultimate questions still remained. Who had written them and why?

Izzy stood up and looked at Iam. "Thanks Iam," she said as she tucked the papers back in her pocket. "You really helped me a lot. These poems have been bugging me for a long time. At least now I understand what they mean. But this is a lot to think about, you know, it's kind of confusing. I think I'm going to go back to my room and try to figure all this out."

Iam leaned forward and smiled at Izzy. "Thank you for asking me to help Isabella," he answered. "They are wonderful poems and I enjoyed sharing them with you."

Izzy turned around to leave. "Thanks again," she said. "I'll see you soon, if that's okay."

"Anytime Isabella," Iam replied.

Izzy walked down the gravel path nearly to the bridge before she noticed Gabriel walking beside her. She turned back toward the cabin but Iam waved her on. "Take Gabriel with you," he called. "You'll hurt his feelings if he doesn't get to go along."

Izzy waved and she and Gabriel started back down the trail toward Exeter. Izzy was lost in her thoughts as she hiked down the trail, her head down, hardly paying any attention to where she was going. Finally, Gabriel barked and Izzy looked up, surprised to find herself on top of the small hill near Iam's woodpile. Gabriel barked again and jogged over to the pile of wood. "Okay," Izzy laughed. "Grab yourself a stick."

Gabriel barked triumphantly and picked up a huge stick. "Come on!," Izzy cried, "I'll break my arm if I try to throw that thing!"

Gabriel set down his prize and picked up a small stick from the pile. Bouncing and barking, he brought the stick to Izzy and she tossed it down the hill. He raced off after it as Izzy started down the trail. Gabriel met her at the bottom of the hill and Izzy obediently threw the stick for him again. The game continued as Izzy hiked along except for a short break when Gabriel took a detour to go for a swim in the river. The last throw landed at the bottom of the hill below the gate. Gabriel grabbed the stick and then sat down to wait as Izzy came up the trail.

Izzy stopped in front of him and took the stick from his mouth. "Can't go any farther can you boy?" she said. She knelt down and hugged him and then patted him on the head. "Don't worry. I'm going to come and see you a lot now. I have to go home for Christmas break but I'll come see you as soon as I get back." She patted his head again and turned to walk up the hill.

When she reached the gate at the top of the hill Izzy turned and waved at Gabriel. He immediately barked, spun around, and jogged up the trail into the woods. Izzy walked through the gate, quietly closed it behind her, and headed across the grass towards the library. The sun was much brighter on the open lawn than it had been in the woods. Izzy stopped, put on her sunglasses, and scanned the courtyard to make sure no one was watching. The campus was loud and busy with people out enjoying the mid-winter heat but nobody seemed to notice as she continued across the lawn. Izzy stepped off the grass onto the sidewalk and turned toward Franklin Hall to go back to her room. But after a few steps she turned and walked back up the walk toward the library. She needed a quiet place to think about what Iam had told her but she was tired of the solitude of her room. The library would be the perfect place since no one would be there on a day like this.

Izzy marched up the marble steps, pulled open the door, and walked into the library. The lobby was pitch black after being out in the bright sun and she could hardly see anything after the door closed behind her. She reached up to take off her sunglasses but unfortunately not in time. The force of the collision knocked her backward and her sunglasses crashed to the floor.

"Oh, I'm so sorry," Izzy sputtered as she regained her balance. "Excuse me!"

"That is quite alright Isabella," Mr. Crandall replied politely. "Please excuse me. I tried to avoid you but in my old age and infirmity I was not able to move quickly enough." He bent down and picked the sunglasses up off the floor. "My apologies Isabella."

"Thank you," Izzy said as she took her sunglasses and tucked them into her vest pocket. "It's my fault. I couldn't see where I was going with these things on."

"I'm glad I ran into you Miss Watson," Mr Crandall answered. "Figuratively, of course, not literally. Might you have change for a dollar bill? I was on my way downstairs to purchase a soda from the machine."

He held the dollar bill out toward Izzy as she checked her pockets for change.

"I'm sorry Mr. Crandell," she said finally, "I'm afraid I don't have any change." She looked back at Mr. Crandall and as she did something caught her eye. She stared at the dollar bill for a long moment and then at Mr. Crandall.

"Can I see that for a minute?" Izzy asked.

"Certainly," Crandall replied, puzzled by her request but too polite to ask the obvious question.

Izzy took the dollar bill and stared down at the back of it. She nearly gasped when she saw it! There, on the back of the bill, was a drawing of the eye that was drawn on the bottom of the first poem. It was identical. She was sure of it!

"What is this?," Izzy asked excitely, her finger jabbing the back of the bill.

"Why, it's a one-dollar bill," Mr. Crandall answered, his voice calm and polite despite his obvious confusion.

"I know it's a dollar bill," Izzy said quickly, "but what's this?" She pushed the bill up toward his face and pointed at the eye.

"Oh my," Mr. Crandall chuckled. "Please forgive my confusion. Of course you know it's a dollar bill. Let me have a closer look Isabella." He put on his reading glasses and bent down to examine the bill.

"That is the All-Seeing Eye," he answered quickly.

"The what?," Izzy asked.

"The All-Seeing Eye," Mr. Crandall replied. "Many historians believe it is a type of Masonic symbol, an insignia of a secret society known as the Order of the Freemasons. But other historians discount that theory. Whichever is true, the All-Seeing Eye is used as a symbol to represent God."

"What?," Izzy cried, her voice unable to hide the shock and excitement in her mind.

"It represents the omnipresence of God," Mr. Crandall said calmly, "that He is present in all places at all times and is always watching. It was placed on the dollar bill to represent God watching over the United States."

Izzy fought to stay calm as she handed the dollar bill back to Mr. Crandall. The eye on her poem was a symbol of God? This was getting crazy. "That's very interesting," she said. "I never knew that. Thank you Mr. Crandall. I'm going to go study now. I'll see ya' later."

"Good-bye Isabella," he replied. "Have a nice day." Mr. Crandall turned towards the stairs as Izzy hurried towards the library.

"Wait!" Mr. Crandall said suddenly. "One more thing Isabella."

Izzy stopped and Mr. Crandall walked up beside her. "I was curious as to what ever became of your poetry. Have you had any luck with it?"

"Yea," Izzy answered, "I'm still working on it but I've almost got it figured out."

"Splendid!," Mr. Crandall replied. "I'm glad to know that you are still interested in poetry. That's very good. If you should ever need any more help please don't hesitate to ask. I found your poems quite fascinating."

"Thanks," Izzy said, "but I think I've got it now. I'd hate to bother you anymore. Besides, Iam really helped me a lot and I should be able to do the rest on my own."

Mr. Crandall cocked his head sideways. "Iam?," he said, confused. "Who is Iam?"

"You know," Izzy said, "the caretaker."

"The caretaker?," he replied with obvious puzzlement. "The caretaker of what?"

"The caretaker of the school grounds," Izzy replied. "He takes care of the lawn and the gardens and stuff like that. I'm sure you know him."

"No, I do not," Mr. Crandall answered. "Is he new?"

"No, he said he's been around a long time," Izzy said.

Mr. Crandall looked confused. "I have been around a long time as well Isabella," he said. "We have had the same two people working in the Maintenance and Grounds Office here for at least the last six years. There is Mr. Bill Oliver and Mr. Timothy Smith, both nice and very capable young men. I am quite sure there is no one by the name of Iam working here at Exeter."

Izzy's head spun. How could this be? She had seen Iam at school several times, planting flowers and raking and shoveling. Was she going crazy?

"Miss Watson?"

Izzy flinched and she stared at Mr. Crandall.

"Are you alright?" he asked. "You look like you have seen a ghost."

"No, I.....," Izzy stammered, "I'm fine. I'm just a little confused, that's all. Iam must be a nickname or something."

"Yes, of course," Mr. Crandall replied, looking as relieved by the answer as Izzy pretended to be. "When you figure out if it is Mr. Oliver or Mr. Smith, please let me know. I would dearly love to speak to him about poetry. There are so few here at Exeter that enjoy such things."

"Yea, um, I will," Izzy said absentmindedly. "Sure Mr. Crandall."

"Good day, Miss Watson," he said.

"Goodbye Mr. Crandall," she replied.

Crandall turned and slowly disappeared down the stairs. Izzy stood motionless and stared blankly at the floor, her mind a jumbled mess of questions, shock, and disbelief. No Iam at Exeter? How could that be? It was impossible! She had seen him and talked to him, once while he worked the flower beds in front of Franklin Hall and again near the library. He was no ghost, he was real, real enough that she had talked to him less than an hour ago. "Calm down," she told herself, "just relax." There had to be a logical answer to all of this, some reasonable explanation better than ghosts or looming insanity.

Slowly she managed to push the wilder thoughts out of her head as she searched for something that actually made sense. Maybe Iam was a part-time worker and Mr. Crandall just didn't know it? Or maybe Mr. Crandall was just wrong? For a moment Izzy thought she had found the answer but the doubts came back quickly. Even if Iam was part-time he said he had been at Exeter for years. Mr. Crandall would certainly know him. And it was doubtful Mr. Crandall was just plain wrong. His whole life revolved around Exeter and he knew everything that went on at the school.

Izzy blinked hard and shook her head. This was too much. Strange poems, an "All-Seeing Eye," and now this. It was crazy. Her mind was so full if felt like it was about to explode and she couldn't make sense of any of it. The more she tried the more confused she got and it was only getting worse. She needed answers and the only one she could think of that might have the answers to the questions rumbling in her head was Iam.

Izzy pushed open the doors and hurried down the steps, her legs moving nearly as fast as her mind. She turned and marched quickly up the sidewalk and then out onto the lawn as she sped toward the gate. Her body struggled to keep up as her thoughts pulled her along, determined to at last find the answers to the riddle. She paused briefly when she reached the fence and turned to look behind her. She couldn't have anyone see her, not now. No one was watching so she spun around and stepped toward the gate. Clang!

The force of the collision knocked her backward and Izzy reached for her nose as the pain rushed in. Her eyes filled with water and it rolled down her face as her eyes instinctively clenched shut from the throbbing pain in her nose. In her excitement and haste Izzy had forgotten to look where she was going and had run face-first into the fence. She stood for a moment, her head down and holding her nose as the pain slowly faded. Finally, she took a deep breath, wiped her eyes, and looked up at the fence.

It was gone! The gate was gone! Izzy frantically looked up and down the fence but it wasn't there. The arch, the letters, the vines, everything. It was all gone! She grabbed the black bars and shook the fence but nothing moved. She walked up and down the fence several times but there was nothing there. She pressed her face against the bars and stared through them down towards the river. The path was gone too.

Izzy staggered back from the fence as if it was some kind of terrible and fearsome monster, her eyes wide and her mouth open, unable to speak. How could this be? How could this possibly be? She stared at the fence as the scenes flashed through her mind- Iam, Gabriel, the cabin, the woodpile. It had all seemed so normal, so real, but it must have been some kind of incredible dream or strange magic.

Izzy sat down cross-legged on the ground and buried her head in her hands. The last two hours had been so confusing, so extraordinary, that she could hardly think. There were too many questions and too few answers and now her best chance of finding answers was gone, lost behind a gate that no longer existed and leaving her with more unanswerable questions. She sat silently for a long time as a tangled mish-mash of thoughts twisted in her head.

Ever so slowly Izzy's mind began to clear and blurry pictures formed into thoughts. Clearly Iam was gone but she refused to believe that he had never really been there at all. He couldn't be explained away as simply a dream or magic or a delirious vision. Despite what her head told her Izzy knew in her heart that Iam was real. Perhaps that was the true meaning of the first poem. Just because something cannot be seen does not mean that it isn't real. She pulled the copy of the poem out of her pocket and studied it. She read it twice and stared at the eye at the bottom of the page.

A thought formed in the back of Izzy's foggy mind and slowly crept into the light. It grew steadily as she continued staring at the eye until it reached a crescendo that nearly made her gasp. Yes, the eye was a symbol, according to Mr. Crandall a symbol for God. But what if it was also a signature? What if the drawing of the eye was actually the name of the author of the poem? And the author had to be Iam. How else could he have explained the poems so quickly and so easily? Iam must have written them and if the eye was a symbol AND a signature that meant Iam was.......Iam was God!

Izzy's head flew up and she caught the gasp in her hand. No! It was too incredible. It was too crazy! She tried to push the outrageous, ridiculous thought out of her head but it kept coming back, clearer and stronger each time. She continued to push it away, unwilling to accept such an unimaginable thought, beating it back with rational arguments, logical excuses, and dispassionate reasoning. But the thought had a power of it's own and couldn't be stopped by the weak instruments of reason and logic. This thought was different.

Izzy sat quietly. As the reality of what had happened slowly sank in she felt the confusing, tumultuous noise in her head slowly disappear. For the first time since she had come to Exeter Boarding School, Izzy's mind was quiet. She could hear herself now, could listen like she used to do so often back home, like she used to do when she talked to ....

Izzy sat up straight and took a deep breath. "Link?"

"Yes Izzy," Link replied.

"Thanks for coming back Link," Izzy said softly.

"Thanks for having me," he answered. "I'm glad you found your way home."

"You're not mad?," she asked hopefully.

"Hardly," Link said. "I've been waiting for you."

Izzy smiled. "I still have a few questions."

"Fire away," he answered.

"Why?," Izzy asked.

"Because you pushed me away," Link replied. "We couldn't leave you alone. We knew you would need us so we had to come up with a different plan."

"You had every right to leave," Izzy said. "I wasn't very nice to you."

"I would never leave you Izzy," he answered.

"But you did leave me," Izzy said. "I tried to talk to you and you didn't answer."

Link laughed softly. "I didn't leave Izzy, you did," he said. "You tried again once or twice but your heart wasn't in it. You didn't believe in me anymore. Without that, what could I do? That's why we had to come up with a different plan."

"This new plan," Izzy said slowly, "whose idea was it?"

"It was the Boss's," Link replied. "Like they say, He works in mysterious ways."

Izzy thought for a moment. "He did all of this for me? Why?," she asked.

"Because He loves you Izzy," Link answered.

Izzy turned and looked over at the fence. She wanted the gate to be there, wished that she could walk through it just one more time. "Link," Izzy said, "what about Angela?"

"She's fine," he replied.

"I feel so bad about what happened," Izzy said sadly. "She got kicked out of school because of me. Her parents are probably really mad at her and it's all my fault."

Link chuckled. "Izzy , come on!," he said. "I can't believe you missed this one. It's so easy!"

"What?," Izzy asked, completely lost. "What did I miss?"

"Okay," Link teased, "I'll give you a hint. The name."

"The name?," Izzy said. "Her name is Angela."

"Exactly!," Link said. "Angela. Angel-a."

Izzy eyes got huge. "No!" she cried. "No way!"

"Yes way," Link said with a laugh.

"I can't believe it!," Izzy said excitedly. "Angela? She didn't look like an angel."

"What were you expecting? A chubby little baby with wings and a harp?," Link asked. "That's so old school. It was the Boss's idea, you know. I thought it was a nice touch."

Izzy laughed but then stopped suddenly and wrinkled her brow. "I missed the other one's too, didn't I?," she asked.

"Uh-huh," Link said, "but don't feel too bad. Iam was a little tougher. Iam is really "I am," the name He used when He talked to Moses at the burning bush. I didn't think you'd get that one. But Gabriel? That's pretty easy Izzy. I thought you might get that one."

Izzy sighed. "Well," she said, "I get it now. I should have seen it a lot sooner. I could have saved myself a lot of trouble. How could I have been so blind?"

"It happens," Link replied, "it happens all the time."

Izzy sat for a long time, lost in her thoughts. She was happy to be rid of the painful trials and the questions and the drama of the last few weeks. Everything seemed to make sense now, or at least most of it did. But somehow what didn't make sense in her crazy, melodramatic high school world no longer mattered. She was different now, an actress in a different play, and she knew what really mattered.

Izzy stood up. "Link, I'm exhausted," she said softly. "I'm going to go back to my room and lay down. I'll talk to you later."

"Okay," Link replied. "Sweet dreams."

Izzy turned and started towards the courtyard but then stopped. "Link?"

"Yes Izzy?," he replied.

"I'm glad you're back."

"I'm glad you're back too Izzy."

Printed in the United States
94345LV00001B/244-309/A